Christmas Jelly

... and other delicious Dry Creek delicacies

By Curt Iles

Edited by
Ashley Miller

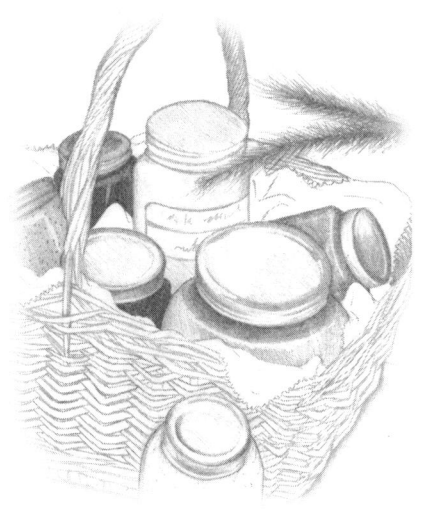

Cover design by Julian Quebedeaux, thaninja101@gmail.com
Title page sketch by Jade Ross

To order copies or contact the author:
Creekbank Stories
PO Box 332
Dry Creek, LA 70637
www.creekbank.net
Join us at Facebook, Twitter, and LinkedIn

Curt is represented by Chip MacGregor of MacGregor Literary
www.macgregorliterary.com

Printed in the United States of America

Table of Contents

Christmas Jelly..2
My Grandpas' Boots...6
Stolen Christmas Trees..14
Santa Claus is Coming to School.....................................20
What it Means to Believe...24
First Christmas in Dry Creek..30
The Best Present..38
A Handmade Christmas (Bill Iles)..................................40
No Room at the Inn...46
New Birth in New Orleans..48
King of Kings, Lord of Lords...54
On Forgiveness..60
Buried Treasure...66
Medic...70
The Warm Glow of Giving...78
The Hardest Day of the Year..82
An Old Feed Trough..88
Too Much Jesus?...92
The Hay's in the Barn..94
The Heavenly Choir...98
Tractor Time...106
A Danish Christmas (Erik Pederson).............................108
Lazarus' Second Funeral...112
A Gift from DQ...116
An Easy Mark..120
Bah Humbug Week..124
The Day After Christmas...128
Master..132
The 100-Foot Line..138
Sharp Hooks..140
Ready to Move Out...142
Finishing Strong...146
Lagniappe: A New Year...148
Epilogue: Honeysuckle..150
Postscript: On Leaving the Piney Woods.........................154
Book Club Discussion Questions 155

Also by Curt Iles

A Spent Bullet
Uncle Sam: A Horse's Tale
Deep Roots
A Good Place
The Wayfaring Stranger
The Mockingbird's Song
Hearts Across the Water
Wind in the Pines
The Old House
Stories from the Creekbank
Christmas Jelly
ISBN   978-0-9826492-5-1

Christmas Jelly is also available in e-book format at
www.smashwords.com as well as other online booksellers

E-book ISBN   978-0-9826492-6-8

Contact information
Creekbank Stories
PO Box 332
Dry Creek, LA 70637
www.creekbank.net

Foreword

These stories are mostly true.
Several are the invention of my imagination.
All are from my journals or laptop.
Most of all, they're from my heart.
I hope they move you.
Go ahead and laugh.
Cry.
Celebrate.
Believe.
Ponder.
Enjoy.

My wish is that *Christmas Jelly* makes this holiday season the deepest and most meaningful ever for you and your family.

In fact, I encourage you to use the stories as part of a family time each night in December. There are thirty-two chapters. One for each day in December, and a *lagniappe* chapter for New Year's Day. Take your time. Like a jar of homemade jelly, these stories are best digested a few spoonfuls at a time.

Enjoy every bite,

Curt Iles
Dry Creek, Louisiana

Dedication

In memory of my maternal grandparents,
Sid and Leona Plott.
My childhood Christmas memories are wrapped up in the gifts of
love they showered on my sisters and me.

CHRISTMAS JELLY

Chapter 1
Christmas Jelly

"The only true gift is a portion of yourself."
– Ralph Waldo Emerson.

With sweaty palms, I wheel my pickup onto Eleanor Andrews Road. I feel as if it's the first week of fifth grade and I'm handing in the dreaded assignment, "What I did this past summer."

Why am I nervous? I'm a man on a mission: delivering a Christmas tree to my favorite grade school teacher. I fell in love with Eleanor Andrews during my fifth grade year at East Beauregard School. The year was 1967 and I was an eleven-year-old skinny country boy with big ears.

She was a legendary teacher who'd tutored two generations of Dry Creek and Sugartown children. Mrs. Andrews was from what we called the "Old School." She had a well-deserved, fierce reputation of being stern and taking no gruff or lip from anyone.

Young teachers knew not to park in her space. Young students knew not to back-talk her. I saw several get a good shaking when they tried.

Everyone knew not to disturb her during her smoke break in the teacher's lounge.

I quickly saw how rigid her classroom was. Everything was "down the line." She was the captain of the ship, and no one questioned that.

The first week of class I witnessed what her former students called "the stare."

Hands on hips. Tongue in cheek. Scowl on her face.

Her stare could stop a charging grizzly bear in its tracks. I made up my mind to not be on the business end of it.

I also noticed something else: beneath that gruff exterior were warm, smiling eyes. She loved watching students learn and leading them into new knowledge.

I learned that Reykjavik was the capital of Iceland, and it was a long way from Dry Creek.

I learned about subject and verb agreement.

I learned for the first time about the heartbreak of love.

I learned to love writing, and my love of reading deepened. Being the mother of three rowdy boys, she had the knack of letting country boys know it was okay to enjoy books and learning.

And I learned to love Eleanor Andrews. During that year, 1967, she became my favorite teacher. Now, over thirty years later, she still is.

She's been retired for over two decades and doesn't venture out anymore. She lives by herself. We call it being "homebound."

There's a wonderful conspiracy in Dry Creek of taking care of her. Former students take her shopping. Clean her house. Cut her firewood. She's determined not to go in a nursing home, and our community is determined that this final major wish of her life succeed.

During this season of her life, she sits among her beautiful garden flowers, carefully tended by her neighbors. She lives alone in her house surrounded by her flowers and memories of a life filled with teaching and touching lives.

This December morning I received the expected call. "Curt, when you get a chance, drop by. I've got something for you."

"Do you want me to bring your tree?"

"Yes, I'm ready for it."

I know that the best present of the season is now ready.

It's time for Christmas Jelly.

Back in October, I tagged a special Christmas tree for her. Knowing her exact standards in a tree, I carefully selected the one I thought she'd like best. Holding my saw, I walk around it one more time making sure it's the right height, width, and color.

That's why I'm nervous. I want her to approve of the tree. Even though I'm now assistant principal at the school where she taught, I'm once again in the fifth grade waiting to hand in that essay.

I remove the tree from the truck, shaking it for loose needles.

"Come on in. I've been waiting for you." She greets me with that special smile I've known over the years. She makes me feel as if I'm the most important person in the world. That's why she's always been my favorite teacher.

She nods at the kitchen table. "I've got something for you."

I see the basket full of colorful jars of homemade jelly.

Muscadine, mayhaw, even crabapple. Mixed in are jars of green pepper jelly, and tomato chow-chow. Topping it off is a Ziploc bag of her specialty candy: chocolate "Martha Washington's."

My mouth waters at the thought of the hot biscuits the mayhaw jelly will top. The green pepper jelly will adorn a plate of purple hull peas. The chewy Martha Washington's to be washed down with a cold glass of milk.

We visit over coffee in the manner that special friends do. We always seem to pick up right where we left off. That's how the best friendships are.

After two more cups of coffee, I put her tree in its corner of honor. Nodding at her fireplace, I remind her to water it good.

"Curt, it's the perfect tree."

"You really like it?"

"It's just right." We now enter the next phase of this yearly ritual. She reaches for her purse. "How much do I owe you?'

"Nothing. The best deal I ever make is trading a tree for the best home-made jelly in Dry Creek."

We hug and I leave with my armload of jelly jars and a lightened heart. At the end of Highway 113, I pause as a log truck roars by. Emerson's quote comes back to me. *"The only true gift is a portion of yourself."*

I touch the decorated jars and am reminded of what the spirit of Christmas is truly about.

It's about giving.

Giving of ourselves.

Sharing what we have.

Giving handmade gifts that come from the heart.

I'm so glad I live in a place called Dry Creek.

A good place where gifts such as Christmas jelly abound.

RECIPE
HOMEMADE MAYHAW
JELLY

- 5 CUPS MAYHAW JUICE
- 5 CUPS SUGAR
- 1 BOX SURE-JELL (PECTIN)
- 1/2 TEASPOON BUTTER

• STIR PECTIN INTO JUICE • ADD BUTTER TO
REDUCE FOAMING • BRING MIXTURE TO FULL
BOIL • STIR IN SUGAR • BOIL 2 MINUTES •
REMOVE FROM HEAT • SKIM OFF FOAM • LADLE
QUICKLY INTO JARS • SCREW 2 PIECE LIDS
LOWER RACK INTO CANNER • PROCESS 5 MINUTES

From the Louisiana Mayhaw Association
http://mayhaw.org/original/

My Grandpas' Boots

"Son, I notice you're scowling at my scuffed boots. Like me, they've been around a while and have quite a story to tell. You'll understand why when I finish *their* tale."

These boots are *six* years older than me, and I'm almost *seventy.* Their history goes back to the years after the Civil War. That war was hard on my hometown of Alexandria, Louisiana. General Banks and his retreating Union army left behind smoldering ruins in the spring of 1864.

My grandfather, Abram B. Terry, wasn't there. He was a prisoner of war in a New York Union prison. When the war ended, he returned to Alexandria and the destruction he encountered deepened the bitterness he felt toward all things Yankee.

We called Grandpa Terry "Pops." His only son, my father, was seven when Pops limped home from the war. He'd lost his left leg and replaced it with a stout dogwood crutch, and a heart that was harder than the hickory peg leg he now wore.

Pop's full name was *Abraham* B. Terry. His first act on returning from the war was going to the courthouse and changing it to *Abram* B. Terry. He didn't want any name that linked him with Lincoln, whom he personally blamed for the war.

Seventeen years after the end of the war—in the year 1882— Pops was still angry about it and the disaster it'd brought to the Red River cotton country. He disdainfully referred to the previous Reconstruction years as "Deconstruction."

However, an event happened in the cold weeks before Christmas that year that changed his heart and our family's destiny.

In the midst of this post-war economic vacuum, several Unionists bravely arrived in Alexandria. These so-called "carpetbaggers" were treated with scorn and suspicion.

Pop's only son—my daddy—was now twenty-three and still single. Father and son operated a sawmill south of town. On this fateful day in December 1882, the two of them were going to the bank.

Pops, seeing a man wearing a faded Union greatcoat, said, "Hey Bluecoat, have you come back to see if there's anything you didn't burn the first time?"

The man, who was sitting at a checkerboard balanced on a whiskey keg, looked up with a disarming smile. "I don't want to burn nothing. I might catch fire, too." He lifted his right pants leg, revealing a wooden peg.

Pops squinted. "Where'd you lose that?"

"One of your snipers got it on the last day at Vicksburg. They say I was the final casualty."

Pops leaned on his crutch revealing his own wooden leg. "Lost mine up in 'Pencil-vain-ya.'" He hobbled closer. "How far's yours gone?"

"To the hip."

Pops grimaced. "I guess I ought to be thankful for below the knee."

"Mine started below the knee too, but Ol' Sawbones just kept cutting." Bluecoat winked. "Told him I'd shoot him if he went any higher."

"Bluecoat, you lost your *right* laig."

The man moved his checkerboard. "And I see you *left* your left one somewhere up north, Reb."

"Yep, they buried it in a stump hole at Gettysburg. Pickett's Charge. July 3rd, 1863."

Bluecoat grinned. "I guess we're even then." He scratched his long beard. "July 3rd. Was that a Friday?"

"It was." Pops stared down the street. "A Friday that changed my life."

Bluecoat said, "Friday, July 3rd. Same day I lost mine. If I remember—"

Pops interrupted, "I was crawling away from the stone wall when they captured me and sent me to one of y'all's prison camps near Elmira, New York. That's where I cooled my heels—or rather *heel*—for the rest of the dang war."

"Like I said, we're even."

Pops' face reddened. "I lost a lot more than a laig up there."

"I'm sure you did."

Pops placed his right foot beside the Yankee's left one. "What size do you wear?"

"9-E."

"Me, too."

Bluecoat extended his hand. "My name's Plott. Hiram Plott from Illinois. Just arrived down here with my wife and four daughters."

Pops studied the open hand. "I don't shake hands with the enemy."

Bluecoat shrugged. "No hard feelings. It's over on my end."

Pops turned away. "It won't *ever* be over on mine."

That exchange should have ended any chance for friendship between the two one-legged Civil War veterans. But my father said in the coming weeks, Pops would faithfully stop by and harass Hiram Plott at the Yankee's makeshift whiskey barrel office from where he watched the river traffic while buying and selling cotton.

My father remembered Christmas Eve of '82 as unusually cold for Louisiana. Hard times led to low expectations for presents. He never knew how his mother—my grandmother—did it. She scraped up enough money to buy a Christmas present for Pops: a brand new pair of riding boots to replace the patched and resoled *one* he'd been wearing since the war.

When Pops opened the box and saw the boots, he began crying, realizing the personal sacrifice that was behind this gift. Slipping the left boot on, he said, "Fits perfect." Glancing down at the spare right boot, he tapped his wooden leg. "I'll keep that one in case my hickory stump sprouts a foot."

What happened next is why this story is memorable. My grandfather called to my daddy, "Son, let's go downtown." Pops, carrying a tote sack over his shoulder, kept looking down at his new boot. "I can't believe Elsie got me a new boot."

In spite of the cold, Hiram Plott was at his usual spot, drinking coffee and staring across the checkerboard and the empty chair in front of it.

Pops unshouldered his sack. "Got something for you, Bluecoat."

Plott glanced up as he moved a red checker. "Crown me."

My grandfather pulled the new leather boot out of the sack, tossing it against the barrel and scattering the checkers. "See'uns, I can't use the right one, thought you might could."

Plott picked up the boot. "9-E, huh?"

"Yep."

He slipped off his own muddy boot and replaced it with the new one. "Fits perfect. That's right nice of you."

Pops nodded at his own matching boot. "Christmas gift."

Hiram Plott extended his hand. "I appreciate it."

Pops didn't hesitate in grasping the outstretched hand. "You're welcome."

Plott motioned to the empty chair. "Let me buy you a cup of coffee, Reb."

Pops hobbled over. "You like checkers?"

"Like the air I breathe."

Pops moved a black checker. "Loser pays for the next cup of coffee."

On that Christmas Eve in 1882, the two veterans began their weekly Friday checker match that continued until the first one died in 1921. They never called each other by their given names; it was always "Bluecoat" and "Reb."

They shared boots for the remainder of their lives, but that's not all they shared. Eventually, they shared grandchildren. Hiram Plott's oldest daughter eventually met my father, and as you can guess, Bluecoat's daughter and Reb's son fell in love.

They are my mother and father.

The two checker players were my two grandpas—Abram Terry and Hiram Plott.

To me, they were Pops and Gramps.

I'm their oldest grandchild, born three years after that first checker game.

I sat with them on many future checker Fridays and learned a great deal. They taught me much more than defending against double jumps and protecting your corner. I learned the valuable truth that two men with opposite views and backgrounds can find friendship if they have at least *one* thing in common.

In this case, a boot for the left and a boot for the right.

My *Grandpas'* boots.

Although *My Grandpas' Boots* is fictional, Hiram Plott was my mother's great grandfather. My wife DeDe is a descendant of "Abram" B. Terry.

In honor of these two family lines and my favorite two women, here are two of their most famous recipes.

MARY PLOTT ILES DRY CREEK PECAN PIE

- 1/2 CUP SUGAR
- 1/4 t SALT
- 1/4 CUP BUTTER
- 3 EGGS
- 1 CUP LIGHT CORN SYRUP
- 1 CUP PECANS
- 1 PLAIN PIE PASTRY

— CREAM SUGAR AND BUTTER.
— ADD SYRUP & SALT.
— BEAT WELL
— BEAT IN EGGS 1 AT A TIME
— ADD PECANS — POUR INTO 9-INCH PASTRY-LINED PIE PAN.
BAKE AT 350° FOR 1 HR & 10 MINUTES OR UNTIL A KNIFE COMES OUT CLEAN

My wife DeDe is a great cook with many signature dishes. Her Christmas breakfast, featuring this casserole, is loved by all of our family.

DeDe's Famous Breakfast Casserole

6 slices of bread
1 lb. hot or mild sausage
6 eggs, well-beaten
1 3/4 cup milk
Salt and pepper to taste
grated cheese

Tear bread slices into pieces and place in a 9 X 13 - inch baking dish. Brown sausage, drain and sprinkle over bread. Add milk, salt, and pepper to well-beaten eggs. Pour the egg mixture over bread and sausage. Top with grated cheese. Cover with foil and refrigerate overnight. Cook 25 or 30 minutes at 350 degrees.

CHRISTMAS JELLY

Stolen Christmas Trees

"I know I tagged a tree in this area." My neighbor Mitzi Foreman walks through our Christmas tree farm on a blustery December day.

Saw in hand, I desperately scan the area closest to the highway. "Maybe your tag blew off."

"No, I tied it securely. You don't think someone took it?"

I cringe. All of the other nearby good-sized trees are taken and I want my neighbors to have the best tree possible. However, we're prepared for a situation like this—extra trees are tagged in a remote area of our farm. I walk Mitzi over to a beautiful Leyland cypress in the southeast corner of our field, away from the highway. She loves it and I quickly cut it before she can change her mind.

Later that afternoon, Daddy and I look for the missing tree. He points to a jagged stump. "Someone cut that tree with an ax or machete."

He shrugs. "Someone stole the Foreman tree."

Who in the world would steal a Christmas tree? I just can't quite picture a family sitting there on Christmas morning, opening presents, singing "Silent Night" around a stolen tree.

That's sorry. As my uncle would say, "That's lower than a snake's belly in a gulley."

People *will* steal just about anything. In the gift shop at Dry Creek Camp, there is an ongoing minor problem with shoplifting. Ironically, the most stolen items are the W.W.J.D. bracelets.

W.W.J.D. stands for "What Would Jesus Do?"

Well, I know this much—Jesus wouldn't tell you to steal a bracelet—or for that matter, a Christmas tree.

A few days later, I take my boots off at our front door. Hanging from the Christmas wreath is a scribbled note, "I cut a tree today." Attached to the note, held by a clothespin, is a twenty-dollar bill.

I kneel and lift our doormat. Under it is another price tag, twenty dollars, and a scribbled note. "Wishing you a very a Merry

Christmas."

My daddy, the world's most trusting soul, nails up a handwritten sign each year at our Christmas Tree farm:

"If we aren't home, you can still get your tree. The saw is on the front porch. You can leave your tag, your name, and money by the front door. Now go do your thing."

I love his benediction. "Now go do your thing."

Unbelievably, this system has worked well. We've found that when you put trust in people, they usually come through in an honest way.

The week after the stolen Foreman tree, we noticed another stump. The thieves had evidently returned, or someone else had sunk to their low level. I tried to remember how many circles of hell there are. Christmas tree thieves deserve to be down there with Hitler, Nero, and the other dregs of history.

I told my three teenage sons, "We're going to catch the thieves when they return." The next night about 10:30, my middle son Clint and I see the headlights of two vehicles leaving our driveway. We spring into action, running to my truck and taking off in hot pursuit.

We are dressed for battle—I'm in my pajamas and Clint in his boxers and a T-shirt. We catch the escaping thieves within a mile at the Dry Creek intersection.

It's our moment of truth. I tell Clint, "We've got 'em red-handed now."

There the culprits are—my mother in her van and Daddy in his truck. They'd left one of their vehicles at the Christmas tree farm going to a basketball game. The headlights we saw were when they returned for the extra vehicle.

Clint and I both burst out laughing. I feel like Barney Fife on one of his overreactions in Mayberry.

My wife DeDe is waiting at the door when the heroes arrive back home. After we sheepishly tell our story, she asks, "Well, what would you boys have done if you'd caught up with the real thieves?"

I look at my nightclothes and shrug. "I guess I'd have taken off one of my house shoes and beat them with it."

In the coming week, I try to balance the frustration of a tree thief against dozens of honest families and friends coming to select a tree. A neighbor arriving with a jar of coins to pay for the tree. The excitement of warmly dressed preschoolers running through the trees laughing and singing is enough to put anyone in the Christmas spirit. The fun of letting a five-year-old boy hold the other end of the saw as he "helps" me cut down a tree. As the tree falls he loudly shouts, "Timmbbbeeer." He'll always remember "cutting down that tree" during a Christmas season so many years ago.

A tree is special to a young child as this story illustrates: a local preschool class came for a classroom tree. They paraded off the bus running to the four winds.

Several parents came to help their child select a tree for home. Four of five trees were cut before the preschoolers loaded back on the bus. I put the trees in the back of my truck and followed the bus to school. About halfway down my driveway, the bus stopped abruptly. Teacher Dianne Brown exited the bus. "Curt, one of the little boys is crying and shouting, 'I want my tree. That man's taking my tree. I want my tree right now!'"

It took careful explanation to convince him we were bringing *his* tree to school.

He thought I was stealing his tree!

A stolen Christmas tree could make one cynical, but the joyful faces of children drown out any disappointment. Besides, a thief has to live with himself. That's pretty apt punishment in my book. He or she saved twenty-five dollars but gave up a little of his soul.

The occasional person who takes advantage of us is greatly outnumbered by the folks who are as honest as the day is long. Our honor system works well because of the belief that most people are good down in their hearts.

In life, we must choose a worldview: whether people are rascals or basically honest. There are plenty of examples at each end of this spectrum.

I recall other examples of "trustful hearts" in our community: Don Gray's turnip green patch with a crudely lettered sign inviting people to pick all of the greens they need and leave their money in the mailbox.

Farmer's Dairy and their butter dish bank for people to pay for their gallon of fresh thick milk. This honor system has been in use for years and Mr. Matt Farmer told me it has worked well.

It's true—in life, we find exactly what we're looking for. Our attitude and outlook determine how we perceive the world around us.

We can see every person as a potential Christmas tree thief, or we can see him or her as the person who'll honestly cut his or her own tree and leave the money under the doormat.

It's a choice, and the choice is ours to make.

We can either say "Bah humbug" or "Merry Christmas."

I like the sound of the latter much better.

Matt and Dee Farmer live in the Dry Creek home they built together over sixty years ago. They operated their family dairy, replete with its fresh milk honor system, with sons Ken, Don, and Wesley.

Sugar Cookies
Dee Farmer

4 1/2 cup flour   2 cups sugar
3 t baking powder   4 eggs
1/2 t salt
1 cup butter   1 t. vanilla

Sift flour, baking powder, and salt. Cream butter and sugar. Add eggs and vanilla. Spoon out onto pan then press with flour-dipped glass

CHRISTMAS JELLY

Santa Claus is Coming . . . to School

I've learned this: life is always better than fiction. You *cannot* make up a story that outdoes the truth.

Gordon Copeland sat in my office as I read his resume.

"Mr. Copeland, you have impressive credentials for a substitute teacher."

He was a barrel-chested man in his late sixties. A thick head of white hair and long beard to match it. A hearty laugh. Red cheeks.

"Has anyone ever told you how you look like Santa Claus?"

He laughed. "Everyday. In Florida, I did a good bit of Santa Claus roles. Even did a commercial for Coca-Cola. This year I'd like to make a little extra substituting."

"Good. We always need substitutes for the three weeks between Thanksgiving and Christmas. I'll be calling you."

I'll never forget the first day he worked in the first and second grade hall. It was early December—always an interesting time in our K-12 rural school.

Like electricity, it spread through the hall: Santa Claus is taking Mrs. King's place today.

He wasn't dressed in red and white. He had on cowboy boots and blue slacks. But he was still Santa Claus to these first graders.

My job as assistant principal was coordinating the substitutes. I peeked into his classroom several times that day. The students were quiet as a mouse, working at their desks. This was not normal behavior when a substitute teacher was present.

But this wasn't just any substitute. *This was Santa Claus.*

He had a weapon stronger than any paddle or time-out corner.

They didn't want a bag of switches come Christmas morning.

I mean this is a man about whom children sing:

He's making a list.
Checking it twice.
Gonna find out who's naughty and nice.

20

Mr. Copeland's noontime appearance in the lunchroom created a minor riot. When I set my plate down at the teacher table, one of them commented dryly, "I don't believe having Santa Claus substitute is such a good idea."

I nodded. "It's made Brandon and Willie behave in Mrs. King's Class."

"That's a miracle. But it's made the other hundred students crazy."

Mr. Copeland became a frequent sub during that Christmas season. The reaction was always the same. His class was on their best behavior, but the other students couldn't concentrate with Santa Claus next door or down the hallway.

Gordon Copeland also substituted in the upper grades. They weren't true believers and didn't respond with quite the same level of respect or awe.

He became my friend during that year and served our school well.

He didn't return the next Christmas season. He told me he'd take his chances at department stores and malls "ho ho ho-ing" over corralling students in a classroom.

The next year Gordon Copeland died of a sudden heart attack. I still miss him and smile when I recall him roaming the East Beauregard Elementary hallway to cries of "Santa Claus is here. Santa Claus is coming to school."

Merry Christmas, Mr. Copeland.

He knows when you've been sleeping.
He knows when you're awake.
He knows when you've been bad or good
So be good for goodness' sake.

Thinking about Santa Claus' legendary all-seeing eyes, I was reminded of a wonderful story from a biography of the great African statesman, Albert Schweitzer:

Schweitzer related the story of a one-eyed European lumberman who worked near his compound. The lumberman needed to go away on business, so he took out his glass eye, laid it on his desk, and called in his African workers. "I'll be gone for a while, but I'm leaving my eye to watch your work while I'm gone."

He returned in several weeks and was delighted that every chore and job had been completed. He had solved the problem of absentee supervision of his work crew.

A few months later he needed to make another longer trip. He repeated his earlier statement and left the glass eye on his desk "to watch things."

He returned to find work piled up everywhere. Nothing had been done. Dismayed, he rushed into his office to see what had happened.

In the middle of his desk was a large hat. He lifted it to find the glass eye.

As they say, "Out of sight. Out of mind."

Now what does a glass eye, Santa Claus as a substitute, and Christmas have to do each other?

We laugh at the Africans and their belief in the magical all-seeing eye.

However, there is a true all-seeing eye. It's called God.

We believe he is everywhere so he sees all. Omnipresent.

Knows all. Omniscient.

He is all powerful. Omnipotent.

Yet, we puny humans think we can put a hat over God and go our merry way. That's way more silly than believing in the power of a glass eye.

Throughout the Bible we find the term, "Fear the Lord." There's lots of discussion on whether this means awesome respect, cowering fear, or more. The answer is yes.

We should have an awesome respect for God. He created all there is. He controls all things. His ways are far above our ways.

And we should have a healthy dose of fear. Not cowering fear, but reverent fear. A fear factor that affects everything we do—or don't do. Our actions and attitudes should be seen through the prism of "we will answer before God for 'every idle word' one day."

My personal take on this is that my fear of God is rooted in not wanting to disappoint Him. I love Him. I revere Him. Yes, I fear him. I don't want to be found wanting in my commitment and devotion to Him.

Christmas is always a good time for introspection.

Looking inside ourselves at what our priorities really are.

A look in the mirror at whom we're becoming.

Somebody is watching you and me.

He doesn't wear a red suit or carry switches.

Neither does he have a glass eye.

Somebody is watching me.

If I *truly* believe that, it'll make a difference in how I live.

What it Means to Believe

This excerpt from my recent novel, A *Spent Bullet*, is a conversation between Harry Miller, a young soldier, and Levon Reed, the father of the girl he plans to marry. It's a conversation between two men about belief. A ninety-two-year-old cousin of mine wrote, "I've taken college religion classes and lived nearly a century. Mr. Reed's *A Spent Bullet* explanation of belief and being born again may be the best I've ever heard." Sit back and eavesdrop on this 1941 conversation in a Louisiana pasture.

Levon Reed spat again. "Boy, you might fit in with this family after all." He tossed a loose end of wire at Harry. "Now start making yourself useful."

The only sound was Levon Reed's tuneless whistling. As the last of the wire was rolled up, he stopped. "Harry, I know we seem like backwards folk to a city boy like you, but we're just different."

He pointed toward a nearby lone pine. "Our tap root's pretty deep too."

"Mr. Reed, your tap root is way deeper than mine will ever be." Harry picked up a coil of wire. "I got a question that's been bugging me: What do folks mean when you talk about being 'born again'?"

Levon Reed hefted three rolls of wire on his shoulder. "It's something that happens in a fellow's heart." He seemed deep in thought as they walked toward the house.

"Let me give you an example. My boy, Jimmy Earl, joined the Air Corps. He and I both love aeroplanes, but there's a distinct difference. He's flying in them now. I've never flown in one and probably will die without getting off the ground.

"We both *believe* planes can fly, but there's a difference in our beliefs. Jimmy Earl believes *in* planes. He's willing to put his butt in a seat and let someone fly him up into the wild blue yonder. Me? I just believe *about* planes. I believe they can fly, but I'm not willing to commit."

Mr. Reed pointed to his head and then his heart. "There's a heap of difference between head knowledge and heart knowledge. It's commitment. A willingness to strap yourself in and trust something else or someone. I believe a fellow's 'born again' when he goes from standing on the ground admiring the plane to crawling in and trusting. It's letting Jesus be the pilot of your life."

"Do you trust Jesus like that?" Harry asked.

"Sure I do."

"Even . . . after what happened to Ben?" Harry shuddered at his own question.

Tears filled Mr. Reed's eyes and he sighed. "That's a good question and also a hard one." He removed his hat, wiping his forehead. "I've been trusting Jesus all of my life. I've trusted him with all I've got, including my family. I can't get my arms around why God let Ben die—been talking to the Lord about it—haven't got a good answer yet."

"Do you think God caused the accident?" Harry said.

"Heck, no. A boy chasing a dog ran out in front of a moving truck. That's what caused it. I don't believe God caused it, but I do believe he allowed it. And I trust him *in spite* of my son dying."

"How do I get that kind of faith?"

"I believe you're getting it."

"But I haven't . . . I haven't felt any fireworks go off."

"Fireworks ain't a sign of being born again. I've seen folks jump high for Jesus and two weeks later be back living like the devil. My experience has been that being born again happens in an instant, but becoming a true follower of Jesus—growing to be like him—is a lifetime process."

Harry kicked at a clod of dirt. "I can feel some changes, but there's a lot more needed."

"It's a process. It doesn't happen overnight. Let me see . . . ." Pulling his pliers out, Mr. Reed clipped off the wire. "Son, let me think about how to best describe this growth process."

The old farmer walked in silence for the next minute. "I was in the Great War. When my unit went across the Atlantic—The Big Pond—I studied that big ocean liner, and watched how they adjusted course. It wasn't all at once. It was more a matter of the captain bumping—or nudging—that rudder a wee bit at a time. Crossing the ocean on a liner isn't made with 180-degree turns, but steady bumps on the wheel. Same thing's true in life-change. Often it's a series of gradual changes that determine a man's course and direction."

As Luke recorded in Acts 16:30-31, " . . . he then brought them out and asked, "Sirs, what must I do to be saved?"

They replied, "*Believe* in the Lord Jesus, and you will be saved. . . ."

Belief in Jesus. It's an action word.

CHRISTMAS JELLY

My Nana and Papa were a central part of my growing
up experience. Living next door to us, they provided many
opportunities for us to pick veggies from the garden and be in the
kitchen when those veggies were cooked. Sunday dinners along
with holiday dinners were a special time for all the brothers,
sisters, grandkids, and later, the great-grandkids, to come together
and fellowship around a meal made by Nana. These were two of
our favorite recipes that Nana never left out of those family meals.

-Robin Mitchell Iles

Potato Casserole

2 lbs. frozen hash brown potatoes
½ cup melted butter
1 can cream of chicken soup
2 cups grated cheddar cheese
½ cup chopped onion
2 cups sour cream
1 t salt
¼ t pepper

Thaw potatoes and combine with all other
ingredients, mixing thoroughly. Put into a well-
greased baking dish, 3 quarts or larger, and top
with 2 cups crushed cornflakes and ¼ cup melted
butter. Bake at 350 for 45 minutes or until potatoes
are done.
"Aunt Joyce shared this recipe many years ago.
Aren't we glad! Sunday and Christmas dinners
wouldn't be complete without these potatoes.
A kids' favorite!"

Spoon Rolls

1 pkg. dry yeast
2 cups very warm water
1½ sticks butter or margarine
¼ cup sugar
1 egg
4 cups self-rising flour

Place yeast in warm water. Melt butter or margarine; cream with sugar in large bowl. Add beaten egg. Add dissolved yeast to creamed mixture. Add flour and stir until well mixed. Place in air-tight bowl and keep in refrigerator until needed. To cook, drop by spoonfuls into well-greased 2½ inch muffin tins. Bake 20 minutes at 350 degrees.

CHRISTMAS JELLY

First Christmas in Dry Creek

J.J. Miller had set up camp where he had a good view of the surrounding area. There were no signs of any settlers in the last mile he'd come, for he had scouted down to the nearby creek and seen no recent signs of human habitation.

It was December 24, 1853, and he didn't expect trouble on Christmas Eve, but a stranger in these woods couldn't be too careful. He'd come down from South Carolina had experienced his share of difficulty along the way. He hoped his sojourn here in Louisiana would be easier.

At least the Deep South cold wasn't unbearable. Back home on the East Coast, the weather could be brutal in early winter, but so far, it'd been fairly nice here.

A pot of coffee perked on the fire, as the twenty-five-year-old Miller sat down beside a large beech with his loaded musket leaning against the tree.

His horse's snorting was the first sign of approaching company. This alerted Miller, who laid his gun across his lap, partially covering it with an old blanket. He soon saw a man on a horse coming up out of the creek bottom. The easy manner the man sat on the horse didn't seem like trouble, but Miller knew better than to relax.

He recalled stories he'd heard on the Natchez Trace about the area he now was in. It was called "The Outlaw Strip" and served as a haven for men wishing to live outside the law in nearby Texas or eastern Louisiana.

The approaching rider must have seen the rifle across Miller's lap. He slowed his horse to a slow gait and raised his free hand in a friendly gesture. His other gloved hand was on the reins. Miller saw no visible weapon so he stood to his feet, holding his gun in the crook of his arm.

Miller judged the older man to be about sixty. He also took note of his tone of voice. It had the same musical quality common among the Scot-Irish he'd left behind in the Carolinas. "Evening, Sir. How are you?"

"I'm jes' fine. You mind if I get off my horse for a visit?"

"Help yourself." Miller did something he hadn't planned to do—he leaned his gun against the tree and walked toward the dismounting rider.

The man walked up to Miller, taking off his right glove and extending his hand. "I'm Burkitt Lindsey."

"My name's John James Wilson Miller, lately of South Carolina."

"Came a ways, didn't you?"

"Sure did." Miller noted the man's strong grip as he asked, "What do you call this place here?"

"We call it Dry Creek." The rider nodded behind him. "That creek is called Dry Creek."

"Is it dry?"

"Never. I was told its Indian name was 'Beautiful Creek' and the English translation got buggered up."

Miller laughed and so did the other man. "Now say your name again."

"It's Lindsey. Burkitt Lindsey. You by yourself?"

"I am. I'm looking for a place to settle where there's plenty of room and a good creek to put in a water mill."

"There's plenty of space for sure around here." Lindsey pointed toward the creek. "There's several places down Dry Creek that might work well. Now what was your name again?"

"John James Wilson Miller," the younger man answered, "but I go by 'J.J.'"

"That's a mighty long name for a fellow as young as you are." The older man's eyes twinkled as he said it.

Miller looked toward the creek bottom. "Is that where you live, Mr. Lindsey?"

"Me, my wife, and our kids live across the creek about a quarter."

Miller noticed the visitor's stare as he hesitated before asking, "Mr. Miller, do you know what tomorrow is?"

"I believe it's Christmas Day."

"You're right. Do you have plans?"

Miller grinned toward his meager campsite. "Does it look like it?"

"Good. That means you'll have Christmas dinner with us. No one should be alone on Christmas Day."

The younger man hesitated, "I'm afraid I'd be a bother—and you'd need to ask your wife."

"We'd be honored if you'd join us."

"I'm not sure."

"But I am. We'll be looking forward to your visit." As if the matter was settled, Lindsey walked to his horse. "When you get down to the creek tomorrow, just ford it and follow the trail up through the hardwoods; when you get back in the pines, you'll be near our place."

Clicking to his horse, he turned back toward the creek. "It was good meeting you, Mr. Miller."

"You can call me J.J."

"Good meeting you, J.J. Miller. We'll see you for dinner tomorrow."

"Thank you kindly, Mr. Lindsey."

"It's Burkitt," the older man answered.

"Thank you, Burkitt, and Merry Christmas."

"Merry Christmas to you, Son."

Miller watched the man ride off into the gathering darkness before tossing another pine knot on the fire. It sizzled and sputtered as he said aloud, "I believe I might be able to like this place."

The next day John James W. Miller crossed Dry Creek and joined the Burkitt Lindsey family for Christmas dinner. It began the friendship between these two homesteading families that now has stretched into its third century. He fell in love with, and later married, Burkitt Lindsey's daughter, Laura Francine.

Southwestern Louisiana is full of the descendants of these two pioneer families that still carry their good names in the piney woods.

The hospitality of the Lindsey family is indicative of what I love best about our area and its people. It's shown in kindness to the stranger, a willingness to extend a hand of welcome to a newcomer. In the unforgettable days after Hurricane Katrina ravaged New Orleans as thousands of evacuees poured into our area, this same hospitality was extended to those strangers in need.

Three weeks later, when Hurricane Rita destroyed much of our area, these same qualities of aiding neighbors, self-reliance, and perseverance stood in good stead in Southwest Louisiana. The actions of people in our area didn't make the national news but we didn't expect to—folks just did what Burkitt Lindsey did on that long ago Christmas—they "crossed the creek" and took care of their neighbors. No one waited on the government or some agency to come rescue them; they banded together, reached out, and helped each other out.

That attitude is really what Christmas is all about: hospitality, service, and kindness as we celebrate the birth of the Savior Jesus who exemplifies everything about giving and sacrifice.

The following three recipes come from members of the J.J. Miller and Burkitt Lindsey families. Their roots run deep in Dry Creek. This steadfast sense of history and place is one of things I love best about our part of Louisiana.

Juanita Miller Brumley writes lovingly of her parents, Jay and Corine Miller, and their Southern hospitality to guests:

Our family rarely observed Sunday dinner alone. Relatives came home on long weekends from Crossett, Arkansas, Port Arthur, Texas, and Lake Charles. On many occasions, the company was visiting preachers and/or evangelists making appearances for revivals.

Mother had her Sunday dinner cooked before she started breakfast. Regardless of who was visiting, she never used company as an excuse to stay home from church.

Our company either stayed home or frequently accompanied us to church.

Martin O. Massinger, president of Dallas Bible Institute, was a fairly frequent guest, along with Mother's first cousin, Reverend William Seth Baggett, who was a pastor at Dry Creek Independent Congregational Church (now Dry Creek Bible Church).

The main course would be enjoyed, then came dessert— Mother's Lemon Meringue Pie.

As Daddy was slicing the pie, Brother Massinger remarked how beautiful and delicious the meringue looked.

I leaned forward in my chair. "Daddy calls that 'cow-salve.'"

Daddy quickly shot me "the look."

I melted back in my chair for the remainder of the meal.

Lemon Meringue Pie
Corine Miller

Pie Crust:

1½ c flour   6 T shortening
½ t salt   2½ T cold water

Combine ingredients. Roll between two pieces of wax paper. Peel off one sheet of paper. Fit crust into pie pan, fluting edges. Prick sides and bottom of crust with fork. Bake 475° about 8-10 minutes. Cool before adding pie filling.

Pie Filling:

1 c sugar   1 c boiling water
3 T cornstarch   3 egg yolks
3 T flour   rind of one lemon
½ t salt   ¼-⅓ c lemon juice
½ c cold water   1 T butter

Mix in a saucepan sugar, cornstarch, flour and salt. Blend in cold water. Stir in boiling water. Cook over medium heat, stirring until thickened. Use some of the hot mixture and beat egg yolks into it. (HINT: Using a hand-held strainer, strain the egg yolks in a small bowl. You will get a smoother filling.) Add yolk mixture, lemon rind, lemon juice and butter to the saucepan. Cook until clear and thick. Cool somewhat before pouring into baked, cooled pie shell. Top with meringue. Bake at 350° until golden.

Meringue:

3 egg whites   ¾ c water
1 t vanilla   ⅓ c sugar

Beat egg whites and vanilla until fluffy and stiff. Set aside. In a small saucepan, combine water and sugar. Cook over medium heat, stirring until thick. While beating egg whites, slowly add hot mixture. Pour onto pie, sealing meringue around edges of pie.

Frank and Versie Welborn Miller were two of my favorite Dry Creekers. Each of them had a pet saying. Mr. Frank's was "Keep it between the ditches" and Mrs. Versie always said, "Bless your sweet heart." Their graves in Dry Creek Cemetery feature each of their respective sayings.

7-Up Cake
Versie Welborn Miller

For Cake:
- 3 sticks butter or oleo
- 3 c sugar
- 5 eggs
- 3 c flour
- 3 T lemon flavor
- 3/4 c 7-Up

For Glaze:
- 2 c confectioner's sugar
- 5 T lemon juice

Put butter or oleo in a bowl. Add sugar and cream together well. Add eggs one at a time, beating well after each egg. Add flour and lemon flavor. Fold in 7-Up. Pour into well-greased loaf pan. Bake at 325° for 1-1¼ hours.

When cake is cooked, let cool in pan at least 10 min. Then while still hot, remove from pan and glaze with confectioner's sugar and lemon juice.

NOTE: I find the cake holds to the side of the pan better if you just grease the bottom of the pan.

If you asked me, "What's one of your favorite things about your church?" I'd include, "Rose Manuel's laugh."

Rose and her husband Dan are special members of our community. She taught an entire generation of East Beauregard students who still love her deeply.

Christmas Meatballs
Rose Miller Manuel

Meatballs:
- 1 lb hot sausage
- 1 lb mild sausage
- 2 eggs
- 3/4 c Italian Bread Crumbs

Mix together and make into small meatballs. Place on greased cookie sheet and bake at 400° for 15 minutes.

Sauce:
- 1 c catsup
- 1 T vinegar
- 2 T soy sauce
- 1/4 c water

Combine and pour over meatballs. Simmer 30 minutes before serving.

* Meatballs can be cooked ahead of time and stored in gallon freezer bags until ready to use.

The Best Present

It seemed to be the worst Christmas present ever as I unwrapped it.

I now value it as the best I've received.

It was Christmas 1973. I was a seventeen-year-old high school senior.

The present was from my Uncle Bill.

Always my favorite uncle.

He still is.

I held the cheap brown booklet in my hand, wondering what it was. I flipped it open. It was a blank journal.

There was a handwritten note to me, encouraging me to write about my life.

Here's a portion of what he wrote.

> *Write about the things that turn you on—the things you like, and the things you love. And also write about the pain you see and feel—the things that upset you or disturb you. In writing these things down in this, your little book, you will be discovering parts of yourself that lie deep within, next to the soul of your being. . . .*

I still have the original note.

It's still tucked in the journal.

It's still the best Christmas present I've ever received.

That first journal sets next to the fifty-eight finished ones.

Thanks Uncle Bill.

Most of all, thanks for always believing in me.

Even when I didn't believe in myself.

That's what favorite uncles do.

A copy of Uncle Bill's Christmas note is located in the appendix.

CHRISTMAS JELLY

Not only is Bill Iles a wonderful uncle and renowned artist, he is also a gifted writer. This Christmas narrative is an example of his descriptive style of writing.
Enjoy.

A Handmade Christmas

By *Bill Iles*

The headache kicked in as I was standing in line at the K-Mart checkout counter. The line was being held up while the cashier checked on the price of a Teenage Mutant Ninja Turtle for the lady in front of me. Behind me two nagging children were pleading with their mother for a Disco Barbie and Super Mario Brothers.

Over the intercom Muzak was playing a generic, unending version of "The Little Drummer Boy," occasionally interrupting it for a Blue Light Special, then continuing the bland song to no one's discernible notice. I finally made it through the checkout and left the drone of the music, the strident voices of the shoppers, the whining children, and the harsh glare of the fluorescent lights behind. I walked out into the cool, dark December evening.

As I walked to my truck another Christmas came to mind. The memory was in marked contrast to my K-Mart visit. The year was 1948 and the place was a house near Dry Creek. I was only five years old at the time, but that Christmas remains fixed in my heart and mind, not for gifts given or received, but for something more singular and sustaining.

At that time the nine other members of my family peopled my immediate world. Frank and Dosia Iles were my grandparents. We called them Pa and Doten. Our parents were Lloyd and Pearl Iles. Clayton, the oldest of the five children, was a freshman in high school. Lloydell and Marjorie Nell were in junior high and JoAnn, the baby of the family, was less than a year old that December. Rounding out our family was my grandmother's sister, Louise Wagnon. We called her Aunt Lou. She was single and like my grandfather, a schoolteacher.

We all lived in a sprawling house built by my great-grandfather long before I was born. The house was located at the end of a mile-long red clay road that connected us to the main gravel road that led on two miles to Dry Creek and some twenty-five miles or so further to DeRidder. Those were the narrow limits of my world in 1948.

It was the year Clayton, Lloydell, and Marjorie firmly resolved to make all of our own decorations from things found in nature. The idea most probably stemmed from Aunt Lou. On chilly December afternoons she would take us on long outings in the woods behind the house to come home laden with boughs of holly, pine, mistletoe, and cedar. Our pockets would be overflowing with chinquapin acorns, hickory nuts, and sweet gum balls.

We fashioned wreaths and autumnal bouquets with the green boughs tied with bits of shiny red ribbon and hung them with gay abandon all around the living room. The room was filled with the odors of pine and cedar. We strung the acorns, hickory nuts, sweet gum balls, chinquapins, clusters of holly and red berries on twine string Daddy saved from Purina feed sacks.

In Big Chief tablets we colored line after line of red and green strips until all the paper wrapping was peeled away from our crayolas and each crayon was down to a mere nub. We carefully cut out the strips and they formed colorful links to a paper chain when the end of each strip was joined with paste made from flour and water. The chain circled the entire room, draped from window to window and door-to-door. Aunt Lou drew Christmas scenes on each pane of glass with shavings from soap. Each scene was connected to some story from her own childhood under this same roof.

Daddy hitched "Old Bill," a wonderfully tame and gentle white horse, to a slide and we went down to a field overgrown with young pine saplings, which he called the "new ground," and picked out a tall, perfectly shaped tree. With a few quick strokes from his crosscut saw the tree was down and on the wood slide. The clinking of the trace chains, as Old Bill struck an easy gait with the light load, seemed to my young ears, what jingle bells might sound like. Laughter echoed through the pines as we brought our trophy home.

The tree was positioned in the southwest corner of the living room with the aid of some guide wires made of baling wire.

Perching precariously on the top of the tree was a large star Clayton or Lloydell had fashioned out of cardboard and covered with silver foil. The few store-bought decorations we used from year to year consisted of a dozen glass balls of random colors, a blue glass bird with a broken beak, and a scratchy silver rope that never seemed to reach around the tree enough times, regardless of the number of different ways we tried it.

We also used the same icicles from year to year. (They were thicker and more durable than today's version.) The method of putting the icicles on the tree always touched off a clash of wills between Aunt Lou and Lloyd. I guess you could call Aunt Lou something of an "icicle purist." She insisted that we take our time and hang them one strand at a time.

Daddy, who hated anything tedious unless it was something he was directly interested in, adopted the rather casual approach of taking generous handfuls and hurling them toward the topmost branches and letting the silver strands fall where they may. Because Aunt Lou was extremely strong willed and at the same time very patient, we usually followed her lead in the "icicle war" but our Daddy never left the field of battle without letting us know that our "nitpicking with those damn icicles" sure gave him the "willies."

On the Saturday before Christmas, Pa took the kids to DeRidder in his olive-drab green Ford for one splendid day of Christmas shopping. He gave each child $5 to buy nine gifts. The two stores that we spent most of the day in were Morgan & Lindsey's Variety Store and McGrede's Five and Dime. The challenge was to buy just the right gift without bumping into the person you were buying the gift for. This was no small task in light of the fact there were four excited, wide-eyed Iles kids meandering in and out both stores at the same time.

Secrecy was the order of the day. All packages were hidden in the turtle hull, under the seats, in the globe compartment, in coat pockets and in Pa's brown leather brief case for the trip home. Somehow we managed to get them all home where they were stashed in closets and under beds until they could be wrapped in seclusion. A deceptively wrapped gift could keep a brother or sister guessing on the wrong track for days.

Our anticipation reached fever pitch on Christmas Eve. After weeks of planning, gathering, coloring, cutting, gluing, soaping, hanging, draping, and wrapping, the night before Christmas had finally arrived. Music was always an integral part of any family gathering and Christmas Eve was no exception.

Most of the family gathered around the upright piano while Marje played song after song. Doten played the violin and Daddy sang in a strong bass voice and played the guitar. Clayton and Lloydell sang, too. The songs ran the gamut from Christmas Carols (my least favorite, even then) to anything from "Turkey in the Straw" to forlorn tunes by Hank Williams and Jimmy Rogers.

I sat on the faded linoleum rug, wrapped in a quilt, in a room our weeks of effort had transformed.

The room was lit by firelight from a kerosene lamp and the flickering light cast from the fireplace. Shadows danced across the log beams that supported the ceiling.

The tree was surrounded by an island of brightly wrapped packages that would be there for us in the morning. My stocking hung from the mantle.

With the singular sound of Doten playing the "Tennessee Waltz" on her violin, I drifted off to sleep in the arms of my mother, secure and warm, knowing that Christmas was only a dream away.

Uncle Bill's mother, my precious MaMa Pearl, was a wonderful cook who showed her love by serving her family.

Cornbread Taco Bake
Pearl Iles

1½ lbs ground beef
1 (1⅜oz) Durkee's taco seasoning
½ c water
1 (12oz) can whole kernel corn, drained
½ c chopped green pepper
1 (8oz) can tomato sauce
1 (8½oz) pkg. corn muffin mix
1 (28 oz) can French-fried onions
1 c shredded cheddar cheese

Brown meat in skillet and drain. Stir in taco seasoning, water, corn, green peppers and tomato sauce. In a separate bowl, prepare corn muffin mix according to package directions, adding ½ can of French-fried onions. Pour meat mixture into a 2 quart casserole dish. Spoon corn muffin mix around the outer edge of casserole dish. Bake uncovered at 400° for 20 minutes. Top cornbread with cheese and remaining onions. Bake 2-3 minutes more.

CHRISTMAS JELLY

No Room at the Inn

They say revenge is a dish best served cold.

It was natural—every child in the church Christmas program wanted to be either Joseph or Mary.

Tom was a ten-year-old and wanted the Joseph role in the worst way. Not only did he fail to get the coveted role of Joseph, it went to a rival of his.

Making matters worse, "Mary" went to the love of his life.

As a consolation prize, Tom was cast as the innkeeper. At least it was better than being a sheep or camel. He only had one line. "Sorry, there's no room in here, but you can stay out in the barn."

He gritted his teeth through the rehearsals, chafing at the unfairness of his role. He carefully plotted his plan for revenge.

The night of the Christmas program arrived. Proud parents and eager grandparents crammed the sanctuary. Innkeeper Tom, dressed in his bathrobe with a towel and belt headdress, stood behind his cardboard door, ready for his thirty-second role.

"Joseph" arrived with great-with-child Mary, and knocked loudly.

The innkeeper opened the door.

"Sir, my wife is great with child and we need a room to stay for the night."

But instead of turning them away to the manger, Innkeeper Tom stepped from the door. "Welcome, come on in. We've plenty of room."

His revenge was complete. He'd disrupted the entire play.

Except for one fact: Joseph thought well on his feet.

"All right, let me come inside and look around."

After ten seconds behind the cardboard door, Joseph rejoined Mary and announced loudly to the innkeeper. "There's no way I'd let my wife stay in an inn this dirty! We'll just stay out back in the barn."

As they say in France, Touché.

CHRISTMAS JELLY

New Birth in New Orleans

It's Christmas in New Orleans, but we're not here to see the bright city lights.

We've brought supplies for Katrina victims. It's been three months since the hurricane devastated New Orleans. The pulse of life and recovery is beating slowly. It's evident our state's largest city will not be the same.

There's a second reason our Dry Creek crew has driven to the city—we've brought Carly back to the city where she was born.

Carly has spent most of her life in New England. When she opens her mouth, there is no doubt she's from Boston. She talks funny *and* thinks I'm the one that sounds odd. In New Orleans, they think we both talk funny. For "Who Dats," to make fun of someone's speech is definitely "the pot calling the kettle black."

Carly and her husband Stan are volunteers at Dry Creek Camp. Once she told me her story, I knew we must take her to New Orleans.

"I was born in New Orleans sixty-three years ago. My father, a Marine, was being shipped out to the War. My mother, eight months pregnant, came from Massachusetts to see my dad.

"She did this against everyone's advice, including her doctor's. She felt she must see him one last time.

On the day after my father's ship steamed out of New Orleans, my mom went into labor and I was born.

Mother was a young teenager alone with a newborn and only eight dollars in her pocket. My mom and I spent three months in the care of a hospitable New Orleans family before finally returning north.

"I've never been back, but it is a life wish to walk in the city where I was born."

That's why we're here today. Carly doesn't know the name of the hospital, family who helped them, or anything else of her three months as a citizen of the Big Easy.

But today, she's come home.

As we ride the St. Charles streetcar, I think of how Carly's mother must have felt having a baby far from home.

 Another brand-new scared mother comes to mind. Her name was Mary. Although she was with her new husband Joseph, they were alone in a strange city. I'm sure Bethlehem in the midst of the census seemed as busy as wartime New Orleans.

Strangers surrounded Mary when she gave birth to her first child. Just like Carly's mother, she was reliant on the kindness of strangers. The scriptures don't elaborate, but I'd like to think there were those in Bethlehem who helped in the days and weeks after Jesus' birth.

I wish there were a way to locate the family who helped Carly's mom. The original family members are dead, but wouldn't it be neat to find someone from this family that had taken in the New England girl with the new beautiful baby?

Knowing how most things come full circle, I'd like to think that this generous New Orleans family has been the recipient of returned kindness in the generations since 1942. Knowing how family roots run deep in this city, it's a safe bet their descendants are in the Crescent City.

I hope and pray this kind family received the same kindness of stranger hospitality in the days and weeks after Katrina. I hope they were taken in and cared for by folks who unknowingly brought the circle of kindness full circle.

Our day in New Orleans is full, tiring, and unforgettable. We see so much that both saddens and gladdens our hearts. It's obvious the *new* New Orleans will be different, but it will be good.

I'm reminded that only the real new birth can rebuild a "new New Orleans." It won't occur through federal mandates, financial stipends, or good-hearted benevolence. Real progress takes place life by life as people are changed from the inside.

  . . . In the heart.

  . . . In the place where all real change begins.

The new birth that comes from a relationship with Jesus.

Let me close this story with a challenge: that each of us will pull back the zoom lens of focus on Christmas and not leave Jesus as the baby in the manger. Please see the big picture: Jesus is much, much, much more than a child who gets attention yearly in the midst of the presents, trees, and festivities.

He is the Creator.

He is the perfect God-man who lived a sinless life.

He went to the Cross, where he willingly, without complaint, paid for our sins to redeem you and satisfy His Father.

Just as we shouldn't leave him in the manger, don't leave Him on the Cross. Because what makes Him stand above all others is that He is alive. He rose from the grave by the power of God. He is alive today.

You can't really understand about the manger without also seeing the cross and the empty tomb.

The words of the Apostle Paul ring true today as ever before:

". . . if you confess with your mouth that 'Jesus is Lord' and believe in your heart that God has raised Him from the dead, you will be saved" (Romans 10:9).

If you've never done it before, why don't you give God a great Christmas present this year? Right now announce that Jesus is Lord by inviting Him into your heart to be "Boss and Savior" and telling Him that you believe He rose from the dead and is alive today.

It's a "decision of new birth" that you don't have to come to New Orleans to experience.

When I think of a committed couple who've stood the test of time, Riley and Troy Martin come to mind. They've been role models in the Grant/Arkadelphia communities for a lifetime. The Martin family is known for its hard work, hospitality, and kindness.

Each Christmas they erect a nativity scene in their front yard with an lighted sign, "Happy Birthday Jesus."

Mrs. Troy's syrup cookies are famous far and wide.

Syrup Cookies
Troy Martin

Mix in large dish pan:

2 c sugar
1 c melted shortening
4 c cane syrup
4 eggs
½ c milk

Mix in another large dishpan:

13½ c self rising flour
2 t cinnamon
1½ t cloves
1½ t ginger

Combine flour mixture with wet mixture, mix well. Grease cookie sheet. Ball up like biscuits, place on cookie sheet and flatten. Cook at 350° for 13 minutes for real soft cookie, 15 minutes for soft cookie, or 20 minutes for hard cookie. Makes about 100 cookies.

This recipe was passed down by my grandmother, Verda (Bailey) Martin to my mom, Troy Martin. In the Riley and Troy Martin household you always woke up before daylight, but always to a big breakfast. We usually had homemade biscuits, gravy, eggs and either sausage, bacon or pork chops.

But nothing beat coming in from school and grabbing a couple of syrup cookies as a quick snack before heading to the barn to feed the chickens and hogs and to milk the cow.

Sunday mornings at the Martin household were really a treat, because we got to sleep after daylight before tending to the animals before church services. Sunday was a day of rest.

We were taught by Dad and Mom to worship God, work hard and always to help others. They definitely taught us this by leading by example.

—Roland "Peanut" Martin

CHRISTMAS JELLY

King of Kings, Lord of Lords

My name is Nancy. This is my story of a Christmas I'll always remember.

I had finished my sophomore year at L.S.U. and brought Jeff home to meet our family. Naturally, I was nervous about how my rural Pineview family would act around him. Jeff was from old money in New Orleans and our rural dairy farm was another world to him.

Everything went fine until Christmas Eve. Our Baptist church had a traditional candlelight service. Jeff was Presbyterian and I explained this would be a lot different from the liturgical services he'd grown up on.

I had no idea *how* different it would be on this cold, rainy Louisiana night.

He and I arrived fashionably late and slid into the pew behind my mother. She and Poppa always sat on the "Rob Lindsey" pew, named after her grandfather.

My father was still doing the evening milking at the barn.

Just as the choir sang "It Came Upon the Midnight Clear" was when Poppa slipped in. His flannel shirt was peppered with rain and the familiar odors of manure and wet cows settled in with him. He put his arm around Momma and winked at me.

The children's class played out their nativity scene replete with towel headdresses and bathrobes.

My boyfriend saw it first. Poppa put his arm over the pew back and absent-mindedly inserted his middle finger in a Lord's Supper cup holder. He had sausage-like fingers with ham-sized hands. He grunted and twisted the finger to no avail. It was stuck.

I put my hand over my mouth. Jeff leaned up and tried to help but only irritated Poppa, who leaned back over the pew to get a visual on his predicament. He cut his eyes at me, which only made me want to giggle.

Momma, as well as two rows of young people sitting behind us, realized what was happening. Naturally, they all lost any interest in the program. All were focused on what would later be called "The Battle of Lindsey Pew."

Poppa tried to jerk his finger out but only succeeded in shaking the entire pew. His finger was turning blue.

The highlight of the Pineview Baptist Christmas Program was always the choir's attempt at "The Halleluiah Chorus." Momma always caustically said, "They're out of their league. Handel didn't write it for pulpwooders, housewives, carpenters, and schoolteachers and anyone with a 'day job.'"

Regardless, it was time for their yearly rendition. The choir leader, Silas Moore, shared the story of Handel's historic performance when the King of England—visibly touched by the soaring music—stood to his feet. Since then, "The Halleluiah Chorus" had been sung with the audience standing.

Sure enough, the first notes rang out and the congregation rose. Everyone except Daddy.

He tried to stand but could only manage an uncomfortable lean, his right hand pinned to the back of the pew. About the time they boomed out "King of Kings and Lord of Lords," he sagged into his seat. His finger was pinched and so was his face.

The song soared to its finish and the audience took their seats again.

Reverend Williamson gave a short sermon and prepared to announce the benediction. Relief was coming for Poppa.

The Reverend nodded at Poppa. "Bro. Bernard, would you give our benediction and blessing on the refreshments?"

Poppa jerked his hand in one final attempt to free himself. It was tradition in rural churches for men praying to stand in reverence. Poppa had been tagged to pray but couldn't stand—at least not straight up.

After a pregnant pause, he stood in a crouch. "Dear Lord, we want to thank you . . ."

I didn't close my eyes and neither did most of the congregation. They were staring at Poppa. About half had no idea what was going on. The other half had been watching him closely for the last fifteen minutes.

He prayed a brief prayer ending with a hearty amen.

Mrs. Daisy Crawford eased over from her front row perch. "Bernard, have you hurt your back again?"

"No, Aunt Daisy, I'm hemmed in. My finger's caught in the communion cup holder."

She took a look for herself. "Is that so?"

Momma stepped in. "Wait right here, I'm going to the Kitchen to get a bottle of Joy."

Poppa, red with embarrassment, snorted, "Wait right here? I sure ain't going nowhere."

The crowd thickened as word spread of the situation on the Rob Lindsey Memorial Pew. Poppa whispered to me, "I feel like a damn two-headed calf at the Parish Fair."

Momma, bottle of dish detergent in hand, said, "Don't talk like that in the Lord's house."

She poured half a bottle of Joy on his finger and the pew. But it didn't help. His finger was swollen to twice its size.

Poppa's Uncle Henry unfolded his pocketknife. "Let me help you, Bernard."

Momma screamed and Poppa made a fist with his free hand.

"I ain't gonna cut you. I got this new-fangled Swiss Army knife for Christmas. It's got a Phillips screwdriver on it."

He went to the work on the small inset screws holding the cup holder to the pew back.

Poppa was free—at least from his stationary place. He walked into the aisle, proudly holding up the four-holed cup holder attached to his middle finger.

Momma whispered, "Bernard, you're making a bad sign."

"Helen, there ain't much I can do about it."

I looked for Jeff. He was sitting on a nearby pew, hands under his chin. He was a psychology major and looked to be conducting a study of my crazy family and neighbors.

A neighbor, Fred Lacey, walked up. "I've got my welding truck out back and believe I can help."

Momma, who could get worked up easily, said, "You ain't gonna use no cutting torch on him."

"Miz Helen, I ain't gonna do that. I want to put it in my vise and use my hacksaw."

This led to a discussion among the older men on other theories of freeing Poppa. One deacon recommended a "cold chisel and ballpeen hammer" but Poppa put the quietus on that.

"I like Fred's idea." He shook the entrapped hand toward the back door. "I trust him to do it right."

The small crowd followed them out to Fred's truck. One of the men got his coon-hunting headlamp out, giving a beam of light on the metal vise mounted on the back of the welding truck.

Fred clamped the holder in his vise and carefully put the hacksaw against the thinnest part of the wooden piece. The observers crowded in for a clear view of the surgery as Poppa turned his head away and Momma covered her eyes.

Fred paused. "Bernard, you sure you trust me to do this?"

"I trust you with all of my heart. Let er' rip."

Within seconds, the piece had been cut enough to break loose and Poppa was freed.

Momma hugged Fred and the observers gave a round of applause.

Poppa held his swollen hand up.

The next Sunday, Reverend Williamson preached a memorable sermon from Proverbs on "Trusting the Lord with all your heart." He used Poppa and Fred's story as an illustration. It helped me understand more fully what true trust is. It's a lesson that's stayed with me all these years.

Jeff and I broke up later that spring. His parents had a New Orleans girl picked out for him that was "more at his level." It was all for the best. I'm not sure he'd made a good son-in-law to a burly dairy farmer.

They never replaced the communion cup holder on the back of Rob Lindsey's pew. There's still a bare spot where it was.

I still sit on the pew behind it. I'd give a king's ransom for Poppa and Momma to sit in front of me again. Many of the faithful faces of my childhood, including my parents, have gone on to their eternal rewards.

I got a music degree from L.S.U., married an Air Force man, and we finally returned home to Pineview for our retirement years. I now lead the Christmas choir. In this age of ecumenical acceptance, the Pentecostals and Catholics join us for the Christmas Eve service.

Poppa always said those poor Catholics had a defective gene when it comes to congregational singing, but the Pentecostals more than make up for them. They add some passion and zest to our staid Baptist choir, none more than when we sing, "The Halleluiah Chorus."

Those Apostolic sisters can hit those high notes on the end.

As we begin Handel's masterpiece and the audience rises, I steal a look over to Poppa's pew. I can visualize his burly arm draped around my mother, his hand dangling down the back of the pew.

It's the Christmas I'll remember long after the others are gone.

King of Kings
And Lord of Lords,
Forever and ever.

CHRISTMAS JELLY

My mom, Mary Iles, is a member of what's known as The Dry Creek Posse. These are a group of single ladies—she, Ruth Taylor, Lorraine Ihle, Shirley Wilson, and Lorna Stretton— who are a trip waiting to happen.

When she's not on the road with The Posse, Momma makes a mean chocolate cake. I've seen folks nearly come to blows over the last piece of her Dry Creek chocolate cake.

Dry Creek Chocolate Cake
Mary Iles

Cake:
- 2 c sugar
- 2 c flour
- 1 stick oleo
- 3 T cocoa
- 1 c water
- 2 eggs
- ½ c sour milk (buttermilk is best)
- A touch of baking soda

Measure sugar and flour. Set aside. Mix oleo, cocoa, shortening, and water in a saucepan and bring to a boil. Pour into dry mix and stir. Add eggs, milk, and soda. Mix well. Bake for 30 minutes at 400.° After 15 minutes of baking time, start icing.

Icing:
- 1 stick oleo
- 3 T cocoa
- ⅓ c evaporated milk
- 1 box powdered sugar
- 1 c pecans
- 1 t vanilla

Mix oleo, cocoa, evaporated milk, and powdered sugar in a saucepan. When mixture bubbles, remove and add pecans and vanilla. Pour on hot cake.

* to make sour milk: add 1 t vinegar to milk

On Forgiveness

Forgiveness: the greatest gift to give.
You can receive it.
You can give it.
It's the gift that keeps on giving.

I still think about in on foggy mornings, especially in the winter. It was a misty November morning that changed our community forever.

Five men from our community were carpooling south to their highway department jobs in Lake Charles. A northbound eighteen-wheeler passed in the thick fog. The driver later said he veered to the ditch when he saw the Volkswagen van, but its driver did the same.

The head-on collision killed all five men. Our village and nearby Fairview community were devastated. Five women became widows; several of my friends became fatherless.

Mr. Ritchie Young was driving the vehicle. He and his wife Ruth were close friends with our family. Their sons, Bubba and Paul, were two of my best teenage friends. I watched up close the grief and loss a tragedy like this brings.

Mrs. Ruth has been my mom's best friend for over fifty years, including the forty years since the tragedy. Mrs. Ruth, Mom, and several other ladies make up "The Posse," a rambling fun group of Dry Creek single ladies.

I consider Ruth Young Taylor a second mother. I love her. That love and respect only deepened when she recently told me this story:

"After Ritchie was killed, the driver of the eighteen-wheeler was charged with five counts of negligent homicide, and was in jail for nearly a year. Elaine Young and I went to see him. They checked our purses as if we might be carrying a gun, but we weren't there for revenge. We were there to extend forgiveness."

She smiled, "He was shaking when we walked in. We assured him of our open hearts and complete forgiveness. He shook even more, but this time from emotion."

I studied Mrs. Ruth's peaceful face as she continued. "Elaine and I found out his family was having a difficult time so we bought them a load of groceries."

I asked, "Mrs. Ruth, how did y'all forgive like that?"

"Oh, you can't do that on your own." She pointed heavenward. "It's got to be from the Lord."

You're probably wondering what this story has to do with Christmas.

It actually has nothing to do with Christmas

Yet it has *everything* to do with Christmas.

Christmas is a time for forgiveness.

Receiving it.

Giving it.

Sharing it.

It is the perfect time to examine a list of hurts and disappointments and wipe the slate clean.

Thinking you can't forgive them?

If two women can extend forgiveness to the driver who killed their husbands, can't you forgive a slight from ten or twenty years ago?

You need to forgive. Even more importantly, you *need* forgiveness. We all do.

Here's another story on divine forgiveness that goes beyond human understanding:

Just his name intrigues me—Biggie Spears. He was a legendary north Louisiana preacher. I never knew him, although I'm friends with his son and grandsons.

As a young parent, he received the call everyone dreads. His son had been injured when a vehicle struck his horse. He rushed to the hospital but it was too late. His son was dead.

Biggie Spears then turned to a man weeping in the corner of the

ER. It was the man who'd struck his son.

He went to the man, wrapped him arms around him, and prayed for him.

In his personal journal, Rev. Spears shared, "I never expected to be praying for the man who'd killed my son."

His reaction that day is worthy of his nickname.

Biggie Spears. Big in heart. Big in forgiveness.

God offers this same type of forgiveness to you. We believe that all the sins of the human race were poured on God's Son Jesus at the cross. In other words, your sins and mine "killed" Jesus that day.

Instead of retaliation, God offers us complete forgiveness.

Biggie Spears would probably like the idea that his kind act in that E.R. was a picture of what God the Father has done for us.

That kind of forgiveness is too costly to ignore or belittle.

That kind of forgiveness is as close as your heart and your sincere prayer.

He is listening.

He's waiting.

And His gift of forgiveness has an added benefit—it'll help you forgive another person who needs it badly—yourself. Often we forgive everyone but ourselves. We carry the heavy load of some sin, great or small.

Some terrible decision that has affected your life for ten, twenty years or more.

An ancient writer, Publilius Syrus, said it well, "How unhappy is he who cannot forgive himself."

Self-forgiveness is essential to our emotional and spiritual well-being.

Jesus says, "Whether you can *forget* that or not, I have *forgiven* you. You don't have to carry that load anymore. And by the way, it doesn't really matter anymore. In fact, I am powerful enough and kind enough to take this terrible thing … this invisible prison … and use it so you can better serve me."

Finally, friend, I want to tell you about the greatest gift you can give this Christmas. It's simple but tough. *Whom* do you need to forgive right now?

Who has cheated you?
Left you out to dry?
Put you out on a limb and then cut it off?
That person needs your forgiveness.

Christmas is a time for dropping grudges. It's a time to remind ourselves that "holding a grudge and hating someone is like drinking poison and hoping it kills the other person."

To help on this forgiveness journey, start small:
Recipe for Forgiveness

• Active ingredient: pray for that person by name. Initially, it'll be difficult to even voice their name out loud to God ... but go ahead and ask Him to bless them. You'll rise from your knees with a new feeling. A feeling that you have taken one step on the road of the freedom that forgiveness brings.

• Bake slowly. Forgiveness is a process. You must work through the stages of anger, revenge, acceptance, and remission.

• Stir gently. Write a letter. Tell them how you feel, and then extend your forgiveness. Then tear it up . . . if later you actually send a letter, re-write it and mail it.

• Go to them, and extend unconditional forgiveness. Remember that they need it, but not nearly as much as you need to give it.

• Avoid allowing one ingredient to slip in. Bitterness. It ruins any recipe and harms the vessel from which it pours than the one on whom it is poured.

• While extending the freedom of forgiveness, ask for forgiveness from them. In most broken relationships, there are wounds on both sides. Ask for their forgiveness first. State it succinctly and specifically and for heaven's sake don't use the killer word: "but." As in "I want to forgive you, but . . . ." That's the kiss of death in apologies.

• Also avoid the "if" word in asking for forgiveness. As in "If I've offended you." Keep it simple. "I know I've offended you"

Remember *their* reaction is secondary. You're doing a selfish thing in forgiving them—you're helping yourself.

Whether they accept it instantly, later, or never, is not your problem, but theirs.

Give the best gift of all.

It's called the sweet gift of forgiveness.

Someone is waiting for it this Christmas.

It's the gift that keeps on giving.

The sweet gift of forgiveness.

Forgive all who have offended you, not for them, but for yourself. ~Harriet Nelson

Carrot Soufflè
Ruth Young Taylor

3 ½ cups peeled carrots
1 ½ cups sugar
1 T baking powder
1 T vanilla
1cup flour
6 eggs
½ lb. margarine (Ruth uses ½ butter and ½ margarine)
Powdered Sugar
Steam or boil carrots. Drain well. While carrots are warm, add sugar, baking powder and vanilla. Whip with mixer until smooth. Add flour and mix well. Whip eggs and add to flour mixture. Blend well. Add softened margarine. Put into baking dish. Sprinkle with powdered sugar. Bake one hour at 350°.

CHRISTMAS JELLY

Buried Treasure

I opened the old wooden box and poured out a small pile of old coins, dog tags, buttons, bullets, medallions, and other metal objects.

It's my dad's treasure chest. These items were found by my dad with his metal detector.

Sometime in the mid-1960's dad went on one of his new hobby kicks. This new interest—metal detectors and buried treasure—stayed with him the rest of his life.

My memories of going with him to treasure hunt are filled with cold, windy, winter days at fairgrounds from Natchitoches to Jennings. The hopeful beep from his metal detector would make my heart jump as I began to dig and scrape for that rare lost coin I knew had been dropped on the Ferris wheel back in 1948.

Instead I would unearth another coke can pull tab or the hundredth wad of aluminum foil. We would find coins—mostly pennies and nickels someone probably didn't bother to look for. Most times the coins were weathered, not worth much more than face value.

Sometimes we'd find an older dime or quarter. Coins of this denomination minted before 1964 had ninety percent silver as compared to today's coins, which are primarily copper and nickel.

I loved how this old silver, although it looked as dark as other coins, shone. A quick washing and rub on your jeans revealed dazzling shininess.

The beauty was already there, just buried under thirty years of grime.

Daddy's fascination with buried treasure puzzled me. He dug and probed for years at old home places rumored to have long-forgotten buried treasure. He never found that Mason jar full of gold coins or the rusted box of Spanish silver.

He did find plenty of plow points, coke caps, bent nails, and rusty bedsprings, but he never found riches.

The contradiction was how Daddy cared little about material wealth, yet loved to treasure hunt. I don't think he was as interested in finding riches as he was in the adventure of the hunt.

The real treasure Daddy enjoyed unearthing was young people. He touched hundreds of lives of teens and children. He especially had an ageless easygoing way with teens. They sensed that he cared. His occupation was with the Highway Department, but his lifetime calling was mentoring and teaching young people.

Clayton Iles best liked finding buried treasure in unlikely places. Young people with little shine were the ones he'd work with, love on, and help grow in the Lord.

It was as if he was kneeling down looking at that dirty and neglected coin. After examining it and cleaning it off, there was shining silver where no one else had given a second look.

Recently I received a letter from Emily, a young person he mentored.

"Bro. Clayton was one of the most important people in my life. I just wanted to tell you again what he meant to me and how much he was used to change my life. He would come get me every Sunday morning and night, and every Wednesday night in his van to bring me and loads more to church.

He brought me to Port Barre on a mission trip in July of 1996 and that is where I was saved. I had been through some hard times and gotten into some trouble and your dad never gave up on me.

I loved him very much... when he died I felt like I lost a grandfather and friend. I just thought you would like to know his memory is still around very strongly."

Maybe, Daddy never found the material treasure he hunted. But he found, over and over, something much more valuable and precious—the *unfathomable* treasure of touching another person's soul with the love of God.

May each of us, as we enjoy this Christmas season, remember the words of Jesus,

But I tell you, do not lay up treasures on earth. Rather lay up treasures in heaven . . .

. . . and may we remember that true heavenly treasures always mean investing in the souls of others.

Crooked Bayou Gumbo
Clayton Iles

1 PINT SAVOIE'S ROUX	1 16 PORK SAUSAGE
1 QUART WATER PER TABLESPOON ROUX	
2 LARGE ONIONS	SALT
1 BELL PEPPER	PEPPER
	RED PEPPER
½ STALK CELERY	1 T LOUISIANA HOT SAUCE
	1 BUNCH GREEN ONIONS
3 FRYERS	POWDERED FILÉ (OPTIONAL)

IN A LARGE POT, MIX WATER AND ROUX, ROUX WILL BE HARD TO MEASURE; JUST LET IT HEAP UP ON A SPOON. STIR AS YOU BRING IT TO A ROLLING BOIL. CHOP UP THE ONIONS, BELL PEPPER AND STALK CELERY. DROP THIS IN BOILING ROUX AND LET IT BOIL, STIRRING OCCASIONALLY FOR ABOUT 15 MIN. CUT UP FRYERS AND DROP IN. AFTER ABOUT 30 MIN., ADD PORK SAUSAGE DICED IN ½ INCH SLICES. ADD SALT, BLACK PEPPER, RED PEPPER AND LOUISIANA HOT SAUCE TO TASTE. STIR OCCASIONALLY CHOP 1 BUNCH GREEN ONIONS. ADD THESE ABOUT THE TIME THE CHICKEN IS GETTING TENDER. COOK UNTIL MEAT WILL FALL OFF BONE WHEN YOU PULL ON IT WITH A FORK. REMOVE SKINS, BONES, ETC. TO MAKE GUMBO EASIER TO SERVE. YOU CAN DO THIS BY REMOVING CHICKEN AND LETTING IT COOL JUST ENOUGH TO HANDLE. THEN PUT MEAT BACK IN A HEATED GUMBO. ADD FILÉ IF YOU LIKE WHEN SERVING.

CHRISTMAS JELLY

Medic

"Medic. Medic."

Nazi sniper Unerfeldewebel Franz Schmidt didn't know English, but in the case of the nearby wounded American soldier, he didn't need to. The man's anguished cries were beyond words. *Medic. Help.*

It was somewhere in Belgium on Christmas Eve 1944, and Schmidt had never been colder in his thirty-two years. But he was in a lot better shape than the wounded American freezing to death twenty yards away. In the hour or so since the firefight, the man's cries of "Medic" had become weaker.

Lying just past the fallen American was a German casualty. Schmidt couldn't remember the soldier's name. He'd only been in their unit a week or so. When he first saw the young soldier, he was reminded that the Fatherland was losing the war. When you began sending soldiers this green and inexperienced, you're desperate. *Desperate*—that's how he would describe the German war effort at this point.

The wounded German soldier was desperately hanging onto life. He'd been shot in the chest and leg. Although he moved from time to time, ensuring he was still alive, he made no sounds.

Franz Schmidt thought of how ironic it was for these two dying soldiers to be lying together on the cold ground on the very day before the birth of the Prince of Peace. It seemed obscene—even barbaric for men who supposedly worshipped the same Savior to be killing each other this near their holy day.

He sadly shook his head. *Those two wounded men won't be celebrating the Savior's birth—at least not on this earth. They'll be dead long before dark.*

The morning's sudden battle had resulted in these two soldiers lying close together, blood from their wounds staining the white snow. The firefight had happened without warning in the morning fog. An early morning American patrol had walked right into the perimeter of his unit of about one hundred Germans.

Franz Schmidt had been called forward once the firing started. He was a specialist. That most dreaded of all combat soldiers—a sniper.

In his hooded white uniform, he had crawled behind a log and set up for business. The Americans had withdrawn out of range for normal rifles, but Schmidt's weapon and methods weren't normal. He was a silent killer, using his keen eyes and untiring patience to do his job.

Using his scope, he'd carefully scanned for any movement in the fog-shrouded woods. Ten minutes later, he'd spotted a blur running to crouch behind a tree. Taking quick aim, he'd shot and heard the sound of wood splintering and a man's cry. He wasn't sure if it was a kill or just a 'wing,' but there was no more movement.

Continuing his vigil, the cries of the nearby wounded American began to get on his nerves.

"Medic. Help, medic. Help me."

He turned his rifle on the American and put the crosshairs on his forehead. *It'd probably be a kindness to put the poor devil out of his misery. All it would take is one squeeze of the trigger.*

For probably a minute, he watched the American's contorted face. Something seemed familiar about him. He finally realized it was the soldier's blonde hair and fair complexion. This stranger would have looked perfectly at home in a German uniform.

That was why he didn't fire—at least not now.

Or maybe it was the noise he heard behind him. It caused him to shift his position for a look back. A German soldier in a foxhole was gesturing excitedly toward the western end of the American lines.

Nodding his head, Schmidt twisted back around and saw a startling sight. Walking out of the cover of the trees was an American. His olive uniform against the white background made him impossible to miss. Schmidt twisted his scope. *This is going to be too easy.*

However, his scope's magnification revealed something else: this American was a medic. The red cross on his arm and helmet made it clear.

Schmidt spoke aloud. "What in the world is that fool doing?"

Slowly and steadily the Medic was leaving the safety of the trees toward the open field. Schmidt realized that he was plodding toward the wounded American who lay a stone's throw from where he was concealed.

He cursed softly and tried to clear his head.

Across the open field, another set of eyes looked through the scope of a sniper rifle. Corporal Robert Wilson had been scanning the snow-covered field for the German sniper who'd just wounded one of his men.

"Where are you at, fellow? Just make a move and I'll get you." It was as if Wilson was back in the Louisiana piney woods waiting for an elusive deer to betray its location.

No one was more feared by either army than the enemy sniper. They were the silent killers who struck when things seemed quietest and safest—like right now. This was Wilson's chance to take out an opposing sniper. It was the highest goal of any sniper, right up there with taking down an enemy officer.

He remembered the mantra from training school. *A dead enemy sniper means twenty more G.I.'s will live.*

He detected movement behind a log in the snow. Carefully, wiping off his scope, he watched carefully, trying not to even blink. There it was—a slight motion combined with the tiny glint of a metallic object. He took a deep breath and squinted closer, making sure his eyes weren't playing tricks on him.

Corporal Wilson detected a rifle barrel's outline by the log. *It'll be the last thing that German sniper ever makes.*

Wilson adjusted his scope for the distance of about four hundred yards. Too far for an M-1, but just right for his Remington sniper rifle. He steadied himself—it didn't matter how many men you've shot, it was always difficult to be calm when the time came.

However, before he squeezed the trigger, nearby voices distracted him from behind. Trained not to take his eye off a confirmed target, he resisted the urge to turn.

The nearby sound of footsteps in the crunching snow made him glance up. Walking past him was the new medic in the unit.

Corporal Wilson wasn't even sure of the medic's name. It seemed like it was Hunter or Harris, something that began with an H. No longer than medics lasted out here, it was hard to remember their names.

The idiot walked past the sniper's hidden forward position as if on a holiday stroll. Through clenched teeth, Wilson said, "Stop."

The medic ignored him.

"Fool. You're dead."

Once again, no hesitation from the medic. Corporal Wilson quickly turned back to his German target. He found the rifle and scoped in where the white-hooded German's head peered behind the scope. The German had shifted his aim, and Wilson knew it was now focused on the American medic crossing the open field.

Corporal Wilson's first thought was *I'll get the Kraut before he gets our medic.* However, that thought was balanced against *If I kill the German, they'll kill the medic.*

Wilson looked up, watching the medic's steady progression across the open. So far, no German had shot him.

He held his fire. *I'll just wait and see.*

Franz Schmidt had no idea he was in the crosshairs of an American sniper across the way. He was too deep in thought watching the medic through his scope.

I can kill him before he gets any closer. He's carrying something in his right hand that looks like a grenade. He's probably gone crazy and wants to be killed.

However, studying the medic's face through his scope changed his mind. He didn't look crazy, but had the determined look of a man crossing a minefield. Every forward step could mean death, but still he came.

"Medic. Help." The wounded soldier couldn't have known the medic was approaching. Schmidt thought. *I'll let the medic get to him, but if he takes one step past, I'll take him down.*

Hundreds of German and American eyes, separated by a quarter mile of open field, watched the medic's journey toward the wounded man.

The German sniper had the best seat for what happened next. The medic knelt at the wounded American. Schmidt couldn't understand what the medic said. He was further confused when the American stood and walked past his wounded comrade.

Hands raised, the medic continued slowly toward the German lines.

Schmidt, meaning to keep his vow to shoot at this point, leaned against his rifle's cheek piece and put the crosshairs on the back of the medic's neck—just below the helmet line.

Unknowingly to the German sniper, Robert Wilson, United States Army sniper, placed his crosshairs on the forehead of his enemy counterpart across the way.

Each sniper knew from experience what a bullet from his rifle would do. Whether it was the American 30.06 slug or a German 8 mm cartridge, the results would be the same.

But neither fired.

They both held back because of what was happening in the snowy field. The American medic stopped at the wounded German.

Franz Schmidt, watching from his hidden position, lowered his rifle. They were so close he needed no scope.

The medic took out a small tube, inserted a syringe and stabbed it in the German's arm. The wounded soldier jerked, then went limp.

Schmidt knew American medics carried morphine tubes. He'd collected them off dead Americans.

The medic, of medium build and much smaller than the heavily uniformed German, hefted the wounded man on his back and stumbled toward German lines.

The medic fell twice, each time leaving a bloody indentation in the snow. As he neared German lines, two brave soldiers rose to help and took the wounded soldier.

The American medic walked back to the wounded G.I. He gave him morphine and began examining his wounds. He then lifted his fellow soldier. Fortunately, this wounded man was small and the medic began his long walk back to the American lines.

Corporal Robert Wilson of Sugartown, Louisiana, had watched this drama unfold from his sniper's spot. His attention had been split between the hidden German sniper and American medic.

Wilson had seen plenty of killing in the last six months since the invasion of Europe. He'd seen many men killed, and done his part to win the part. It was now time to add one more shot to the tally.

Lying behind a tree in the Belgium winter, he focused on his target—the German sniper's head. He clicked the scope for the four hundred yard shot. *I can make this shot in my sleep.*

Wilson's eyes watered, evidently from the cold—or maybe not.

He lowered his rifle. *It's Christmas Eve. Tomorrow's Christmas day. There'll still be killing today and even tomorrow, but it won't be from me.*

He took his safety off, wiped his face, and whispered toward the distant German sniper, as if the man could hear him.

"Merry Christmas, my friend,
Froshes Fest."

One of the unique features of Southwestern Louisiana are the two German-American colonies in the Crowley/Eunice rice farming country. The Roberts Cove Germans are Catholic while their nearby neighbors in Mowata are Baptists. Both enclaves are famous for hard-working farmers who built strong families and communities on the Cajun Prairie.

My daughter-in-law, Sara, hails from the Mowata clan. This is her mother's famous eggnog recipe. No Christmas is complete without Helen's hospitality and a cup of eggnog.

German Baptist Eggnog
Helen Lengefeld Knuckles

Serves 6-8 cups
1/2. gal. milk
3 egg yolks
1 . cups sugar
3 tsp. almond flavoring (or rum)
Mix 3 egg yolks in . cup of milk.
Mix well and add to 7 . cups of cold milk in pot.
Add sugar and almond flavoring to milk/egg mixture.
Adjust sugar and flavoring to taste.
Heat thoroughly over medium heat stirring constantly with a wire whisk.
Do not bring to boil or overcook.
Eggnog is ready when metal spoon dipped in milk mixture is coated..
Serve warm with topping of Cool Whip.
Sprinkle with nutmeg.
Enjoy!

CHRISTMAS JELLY

The Warm Glow of Giving

It's the kind of December day Louisiana is famous for: cold and foggy, with a thick humidity that chills you to the bottom of your toes.

I feel kind of like the weather. I didn't sleep well last night and my personal battery needs recharging. Parking my truck outside the Hope Center, I wipe my boots on the back porch mat before fumbling with a balky doorknob. It finally relents to my twisting and I step inside a large meeting room.

This room, which doubles as a bluegrass music stage, is crammed with people. They're manning an assembly line that would make Henry Ford proud. They're not connecting car parts—they're putting food into large cardboard boxes.

These senior adults are the Third Tuesday Food Box Crew at The Hope Center. They're busy putting bags of kidney beans, rice, and other foodstuff into the box. The room is abuzz with laughter and talking. It reminds me of movie scenes from Santa's North Pole workshop the week before Christmas.

Maybe it's due to the cold dampness outside, but there is a warm glow of energy pulsating in the room. The room is filled with light, and it's not the type given off by fluorescent bulbs.

I realize it's the warm glow of giving. These folks have learned that it truly is more blessed to give than to receive. They're filling boxes of food for needy folks—boxes that will make a difference in how happy a Christmas some "shut-ins" and families will have.

The brightest glow in the room comes from Mancel and June Reeves.

Mancel isn't able to work today. Vertigo keeps him from standing without "getting sick-dizzy." In spite of this, he still has that glow.

His glow comes from the inside. It's a joy I notice in the faces of committed followers of Jesus. The glow is intensified by the joy of giving that fills this building on US Highway 190 near Ragley,

Louisiana.

His wife, June, scurries about the room instructing everyone and keeping the assembly line going. I catch up with her near the walk-in freezer. She has that same glow on her face. It's the glow of giving.

Giving, it's just what Christmas is about. June and Mancel are at the age where folks are supposed to sit in a rocker and while away the hours. They're as busy serving others as they've ever been.

I walk up and down the assembly line visiting with many friends. As country people do, they pick at me, "Well, look who shows up when the work's all done" and "I'd sure like to be a writer where I just come and go whenever I please."

It's all in fun and I laugh with them. I am slightly jealous of them as they work in the happy camaraderie of people getting "outside themselves."

But I've been working too. I've brought my own gift. I hand a stack of papers to June Reeves. She'd asked me to write a Christmas story for placement in each box. I've also brought a box of books. One of my books will go in each box. I'm reminded that my hands and hearts are also part of this assembly line—just in a different way.

I ease to the door. I'm speaking to a high school class in DeRidder and need to get going. The Food Box Crew wishes me a Merry Christmas.

It's still cold outside, but it seems as if the dampness doesn't soak into my bones as before. That room at The Hope Center has warmed me.

A room full of the warm glow of giving.

No teacher taught more East Beauregard students than Glenda Hagan. During an illustrious career of nearly forty years, Glenda guided young people in reading, writing, diagramming sentences, and the love of English.

She also boosted morale at our school with a combination of great food and fun practical jokes. (Who can forget her famous Christmas Ex-Lax brownies shared with several coaches as repayment on a previous prank? She also sent fellow teacher Agnes Young a jar of hand lotion that was actually Elmer's glue.)

She could not only dish it out (no pun intended) but take it as well.

She was the butt of my favorite all time April Fool's Joke. I had my co-conspirators, school secretaries Bonnie and Carolyn, call her to the office with this note: *Mrs. Hagan, please call Mr. Fox at 318 441-6810.*

Bonnie shrugged. "He asked you to call him today if possible."
I was hiding behind the door.
"This is Glenda Hagan. I have a call from Mr. Fox."
Her shriek was ample evidence of what she'd heard on the other line.
"Ma'am, this is the Alexandria Zoo. It's April Fool's Day."
Glenda shouted. "Where is Curt Iles? I'm going to kill him."
I recommend Glenda's Fruit Salad recipe.
But be careful with her chocolate brownies. They're unforgettable.

Fruit Salad
Glenda Hagan

10 oz   Cool Whip
3 oz   cream cheese
10 oz   strawberries, partially drained
         fruit cocktail, drained
16 oz   mandarin oranges
10 oz   bag of little marshmallows

Mix them together and chill.

CHRISTMAS JELLY

The Hardest Day of the Year

Christmas Eve is not when you expect to stand at the cemetery. I'm here with my friend, Julian Campbell. We're selecting a gravesite for his sister Kathleen, who died the day before after a brave battle with cancer.

It's fitting I'm with Julian. He and his family helped bury my dad. Now I'm going to help him bury his sister.

I hate death. I especially hate it at Christmas. Death and this holiday shouldn't go together, but they often do.

As a teenager, I learned a lasting lesson about Christmas and death. A member of our church, George Forbes, was dying of cancer. I was home from college and volunteered to sit with him at night.

He'd been insistent that he die at home surrounded by his family. I arrived late on Christmas Eve and his wife said, "It won't be long. They don't think he'll make the night."

Every breath seemed as if it'd be his last. During the night, he roused and whispered, "I've got to stay here to see my boy get his new bike."

The next afternoon, his son got his bike.

An hour later, George Forbes was dead.

When I was two years old, a tragedy occurred in my family. My dad's youngest brother Clint. a first grader, was run over and killed as he left school. It happened right in front of the family home on Bon Ami Street in DeRidder.

Clint, age six, was the youngest of the six Iles siblings. His short life and sudden death affected and shaped our extended family and does to this day. Clint lived among grandparents, parents, and five siblings in an extremely close-knit family.

He died on December 3, 1958. Only three weeks before Christmas. I was nearly three and don't remember the details. I only have a vague memory of knowing something terrible had happened among the people I loved deeply.

I've wondered how Christmas 1958 must have been for our family. How can presents, eating and singing be done in a time when your hearts been ripped out?

My Uncle Bill, who was especially close to his younger brother, later painted a large mural about the day of his brother's death. It shows all of our family in their respective manners of grief. I'm moved beyond words when I see the abstract images of my grandparents, great grandparents, dad and his siblings as they process the news of Clint's death.

My earliest Christmas memories are joyful—fiddle playing, games, laughter, opening presents from the youngest up. Christmas in the Iles family was a time of great celebration and family.

Knowing how painful those Christmas's must have been only deepens my love and admiration for my family.

At age six, I started first grade and was given a set of engraved pencils. *Clinton David Iles*. They were a gift from that terrible sad Christmas of 1958. My mother had saved them for me. I didn't realize what they meant but would give a king's ransom to hold one today.

Uncle Clint's death affected our family greatly, but in many ways the effect was positive. I grew up in a nest of four generations of love, surrounded by doting great grandparents, grandparents, uncles, aunts, and cousins. It was as if the older family member had channeled their grief to love.

When our second son was born in 1984, I asked my grandma Pearl the question I'd longed to. "MaMa, would it be okay if we named him Clint?"

I'll always recall the instant stream of tears that flowed from her clear blue eyes. "I'd love it."

In 2003, my father, the oldest of the five Iles siblings, died. Hundreds packed our church for his funeral. At the conclusion of the service, the Southern tradition of passing by the casket to "pay final respects" began.

As the line snaked around the aisle, I saw Mrs. Heard and her husband. She was the driver of the car that struck Uncle Clint on that fateful December day forty-five years ago.

The accident was not her fault and our family had reached out to her immediately. I've always cherished the story of my grandmother, mourning in bed on the night of Clint's death, sending my aunts to console Mrs. Heard.

As she and her husband approached, I felt movement behind me. It was Uncle Bill, Aunt Lloydell, and Aunt JoAnn joining Mrs. Heard at the casket in a show of support.

She cried and so did I. Our families had been intertwined since that sad day in 1958 and it was borne out again on this day. I'd never been prouder to bear the Iles name.

This Christmas, you'll be surrounded by hurting people.

Many are hurting due to the loss of a loved one.

An empty seat around the table this year.

One less present.

One less memory.

For others, it's been decades since the death of a spouse, child, or parent. Regardless, each Christmas re-opens the wound.

Many others are hurting due to other deaths.

The death of a marriage.

Maybe the death of a dream.

The loss of a job . . . and a nagging hopelessness for the future.

The demise of a dream.

The distance of a child.

Let's be looking for those hurting folks this Christmas. Sadly, they don't wear a placard saying, "I'm hurting. I've had a loss."

Many times they reveal their pain in the strangest of ways.

Rudeness in a shopping line.
A shaking fist at a stoplight.
A cold stare on a sidewalk.
They've got a rock in their shoe. You can't see it, but it's very painful.
Give them a gift. Cut them some slack.
Return a smile for the stare.
A kind word for the gruffness.
It's Christmas.
The most stressful, and sometimes saddest, season of the year.
It's the longest day of the year for many folks.
It can also be the loneliest day of the year.
Be kind. It may be the hardest day of the year
for someone you meet.

Postscript

In my recent novel, *A Spent Bullet*, a young boy named Ben dies in an accident similar to Uncle Clint's. I have felt the wrath of my readers. "How could you let that sweet boy die?"

I reply, "In real life, even sweet boys die. It happened in my family."

Julian and Marilyn Campbell mean so much to our family. We've spent many wonderful evenings in the embrace of music, laughter, and friendship. Marilyn's death left a void in all of Dry Creek. This wonderful tribute by her daughter Kay illustrates how we cherish memories of those we've lost:

When I'm not feeling well, two things come to mind during the healing process: Mom taking care of me and the aroma of homemade potato soup. Nothing could compare to Mama throwing together that homemade potato soup to soothe my aches, pains and upset stomach.

One day as I watched her cook in the kitchen, I tried to observe how she made the soup. . . after all, I would have children one day and I would want to comfort them in the same manner.

To my delight, it took only a few simple steps that assured me that one day I could maintain her tradition. Very few great cooks write an exact recipe down.

Over the years, I've attempted to recreate her special mix. I challenge you to recreate your own soup and begin making memories!

—Kay Campbell Fox

Homemade Potato Soup
Marilyn Campbell

4-5 Potatoes cut into pieces

. Chopped Onion

2 Stalks Chopped Celery

1 Thinly Chopped Carrot (optional)

Seasoning to suit your taste

2-3 Tbsp Instant Mashed Potatoes

Thicken with milk and butter

Boil Potatoes in water and seasoning for 10 minutes. Add onion celery and carrot and cook until soft. Add instant mashed potatoes for consistency. Thicken with milk and butter. Enjoy with crackers.

CHRISTMAS JELLY

An Old Feed Trough

> When Mary birthed Jesus 'twas in a cow's stall,
> With wise men and farmers and shepherds and all.
> – "I Wonder as I Wander"

The old barn looks *snakey*.

You may not realize snakey is an adjective. It can mean "overrun with snakes."

In our area of the South, it refers to any place where you expect to find snakes such as, "don't put your hand in there, it looks snakey."

My pawpaw's old barn has a broken roof, rotten walls, and thick spider webs that may be the only things holding it together.

And it's been empty for thirty years.

During my boyhood, it was full of animals. Two plow horses named Sam and Dallas, calves, woods hogs, and scurrying chickens.

Now it's dark, damp, and lonely.

It's a clear cold day before Christmas. They kind of day PawPaw would've called "hog-butchering weather."

I'm on a strange mission. I'm looking for a feed trough.

Yesterday I read Luke 2 on the birth of Jesus. I've read and heard the story hundreds of times, but always learn something new about the greatest night in the history of Planet Earth.

Everything about that night was humble.

The first to learn of the Savior's birth were shepherds, the outcasts of Jewish society. One more reminder that Jesus' bond was, and continues to be, among the common people of the world.

It is amazing that the most educated, wealthiest, and powerful have a hard time with Jesus as the Son of God. Throughout the two thousand years since that Bethlehem night, He has most often found the biggest welcome among the simple and common people of this world.

Folks like you and me.

God could have provided any place for the birth of His Son, but He chose an old barn.

No fanfare.

No luxury.

That name Emmanuel—God with us—was lived out that night.

It's astounding that His parents wrapped Him in a blanket and laid Him in a manger.

It's a shame how we've cleaned up and sanitized the manger. A manger is nothing but a fancy term for an old feed trough—the very place where a few hours earlier, a donkey, horse, or sheep had been eating and slobbering.

That's why I'm at PawPaw's old barn today. I've come for a feed trough.

In the barn, I find out that's rough, weathered, and filled with rotten hay and trash. It's been the home for my sister's cat.

Well-used feed troughs always have a smell of feed. They are wet from the saliva of a hungry animal. The edges are chewed down from animals trying to get that last kernel of grain.

I begin pulling the trough from the stall wall. It comes loose except for one stubborn rusty nail. After several tries I grab hold with both hands and jerk.

The nail comes out, the trough comes loose, and I unceremoniously fall hard on my butt. I'm lying there with the trough in my hands.

I have to laugh. I'm unhurt, lying in a puddle of rainwater that still smells of manure.

I carry the prized trough under my arm. At the barn entrance, I stop and look around. Remembering how a live barn is: the smells of wet animals. The noise, the cramped surroundings.

My friends who have been to the Holy Land tell about the small caves that serve as barns. It is probably in that cramped, noisy, nasty environment that Jesus was born.

The greatest story ever told . . . and the official opening act begins in a dark, humble barn.

The King of Kings, to be worshipped by millions forever, is first laid in a well-used feed trough.

Then I think of the unique teachings of Jesus, the God-Man.

I have come to give my life.
The first shall be last . . .
Whatever you have done unto the least of these.

I load the feed trough in the truck, silently thanking God for teaching me new lessons this Christmas season.

Lessons of humility.

Lessons of service.

Lessons of giving.

I wonder as I wander out under the sky
How Jesus the Savior did come for to die
For poor on'ry people like you and like I;
I wonder as I wander out under the sky.

Flo Campbell is famous for many dishes including her scalded cornbread and homemade tomato chow-chow. She served as a mother/grandmother/friend to hundreds of East Beauregard students.

Apple Bars
Florence Campbell

1 1/4 C sugar
1 1/2 C all-purpose flour
1 t cinnamon
1 t soda
3/4 c oil
2 eggs
1 t vanilla flavoring
1 c pecans, chopped
2 c apples, chopped

- Blend sugar, cinnamon, and soda in large bowl.
- Add eggs, oil, and vanilla.
- Blend well.
- Add nuts and apples
- Mix well
- Pour into greased and floured rectangle pan
- Bake at 350° until golden brown and a toothpick inserted comes out clean.

Too Much Jesus?

As you've noticed, many of the stories in *Christmas Jelly* are about Jesus.

He is what Christmas is about. We make no apologies for making Him front and center of this book.

Once I heard a powerful sermon by one of my favorite preachers, Jason Townley. As the message ended and crowd left, I shook his hand. "Jason, you did well, but I have one complaint."

His face dropped.

"You talked a little too much about Jesus."

I thought he was going to hit me with his five-pound Bible.

We cannot talk too much about Jesus.

We cannot write too much about him.

It's Christmas. His birthday celebration.

He belongs not only in the center but also at the height.

Far above all others.

DeDe and I have a drawer full of encouraging notes sent by Jean E. Mitchell. She was DeDe's mentor during her teen years. She and her husband David touched a generation of students at Harrisonburg High. Her oatmeal cookies were prized nearly as much as the sweet notes that went with the treats.

Jean E.'s sudden death before Christmas 2011 left a hole in the Mitchell family as well as the Harrisonburg community.

Jean E. Mitchell's
Frosted Oatmeal Cookies

1 cup butter, softened 1 ½ _cups_ all-purpose flour_ _

1 cup brown sugar, packed 1 tsp. soda

1 cup granulated sugar 1 tsp. salt

2 eggs 3 cups quick cooking oatmeal

1 tsp. vanilla

Cream softened butter (or margarine) and the sugars. Add eggs and blend. Add vanilla, then dry ingredients. Add the uncooked oatmeal last. Chill dough overnight in refrigerator or freezer. When dough is cold, roll into balls (2 teaspoons dough per roll). Place 12 balls on a greased cookie sheet (ungreased). Bake at 375 degrees for about 10 minutes. Cookies will spread. Remove immediately from sheet when done. Cool cookies on waxed paper. Brush on frosting when cookies area cooled.

Cinnamon Coffee Frosting

3 tablespoons melted butter 1 teaspoon vanilla

1 cup powdered sugar . teaspoon cinnamon

1 tablespoon liquid coffee

Cream the butter and sugar together. Add the other ingredients and mix until it is of the proper consistency for spreading. Brush on warm cookies with a basting brush.

The Hay's in the Barn

It's "Christmas Eve-Eve."

Two days until Christmas. It's close but there's still time for planning and dreaming.

A strong cold front is blowing in as I arrive at Foreman's Meat Market. Last night we were in shirtsleeves. By tonight it will be freezing.

Long Vee-formations of geese have been flying over all morning. They're honking and struggling against the humid south wind being pulled toward the cold front.

Foreman's is a busy place in the week leading up to Christmas. Customers are gassing up or buying meat for family gatherings. Others are picking up deer sausage.

The first drops of rain come from the darkening sky, and then the bottom drops out. A flatbed truck, loaded high with round bales of hay, skids into the parking lot. Three cowboys fall out of the truck and hurriedly begin pulling out a blue tarp over the hay.

They tell me they're bound for Lake Charles. The wind is now turning out of the north whipping their tarps. They tie down their load and roar south.

Today is a good day to make sure *the hay is in the barn*. This common rural saying refers to finishing a task by a certain deadline.

The hay's in the barn. The good feeling resulting from doing all you can do. You've done a hard job and done it well.

It's a good feeling.

Back at Foreman's parking lot, the rain is arriving in sheets. I've got one more trip to town before Christmas. My hay is not quite all in the barn . . . there are a few more presents to buy.

When Dry Creekers say, "I'm going to town" they mean DeRidder. A neighbor's friendly "I'm going to town. Do you need anything?" is a common question.

Super Wal-Mart. I dread going in there on this crazy shopping day.

I talk my youngest son, Terry, into going in with me. I bribe him with the idea of a burger and fries. That's the best way to get a rural boy to go into DeRidder—let him drive and promise him something to eat.

Driving the twenty-five miles to town, the rain pours down. As we pass Bundick Lake, the whitecaps are surging, pushed by the strengthening north wind.

The Wal-Mart parking lot is full. We park out near the highway and hurry in. The rain has stopped and the air has turned much colder. Shoppers, many lightly dressed, scurry in and out of the store.

Like me, the shoppers haven't quite got all of their hay in the barn. I recall Uncle Bill telling of Christmas Eve at a K-Mart in Lake Charles. He said the hurry, frustration, and impatience of these last–minute, desperate shoppers was something to behold.

I bet tomorrow night will be just that crazy at this Wal-Mart. I'd like to be brave enough one Christmas Eve to come observe it.

Terry and I split up and decide on a place to meet later. I wonder how long it will take as crowded as the store is. DeDe will hardly shop with me here because of how many people I visit with.

Today is different. Everyone's in a hurry. Plenty of "Merry Christmases" abound combined with smiles and good-natured remarks. But there is little of the stop-and-visit normally found in the culture of Beauregard parish shopping.

And I know why: everyone here today is trying to get all of his or her hay into the barn.

After returning from town, I go to the cemetery and drain the water in the public restrooms. I recheck all of the pipes and faucets at our home as well as the Old House.

It's dark now and the temperature continues to drop. This will be one of the coldest Christmases in a long time.

But I'm fine. I've got my hay in the barn.

Before going to bed, I decide to make a personal "hay in the barn" list:

- I want to be full of gratitude at this special time of the year. I want to thank God for each and every blessing.

- I want to enjoy my family. What a gift family is! As my family grows and leaves the nest, I'm reminded to cherish each precious moment.

- I want to spread good cheer. I'm reminded that Christmas is often the toughest time of the year for folks. I want to call, write, and check on them.

- I want to make sure there is no unforgiveness in my life. Are there any walls that need breaking down? What better time of the year than now!

- I will seek to live the regret-free life. I want a minimum of "should'ves and could'ves."

Closing my journal, I crawl into bed.
I sleep great that night.
I should.
The hay's all in the barn.

CHRISTMAS JELLY

The Heavenly Choir

Christmas season—The Dry Creek Church choir sings beautifully in a way beyond description. It's much more than a musical . . . it's a production . . . replete with drama, stories, and best of all, inspiring music.

Joseph and Mary enter the back of our sanctuary. It's Tom and Konnie Humphreys. Tom and Konnie are former hippies and always look the part of Joseph and Mary: Konnie with her long flowing hair. Tom with his long hair and beard, kind eyes, and broad shoulders.

Tom is holding baby Jesus, but it's actually Libby, their infant daughter. He touches me on the shoulder. "Brother Curt, I want you to see my baby son, Jesus."

His emotional introduction catches me off guard and touches my soul. It's as if we're in the first century Jerusalem temple on baby Jesus' first visit there.

Tom's next stop is at Uncle Rob McCracken's seat. He's the oldest man in our church at ninety. Tom holds baby Jesus in front of the old man. "Uncle Rob, aren't you proud of my son Jesus?"

Uncle Rob, in the early stages of dementia, sweetly strokes the baby's hair as he hums a tune.

It's as if old Simeon is at last touching the long awaited Messiah he's waited a lifetime to see. Simeon's words ring out. *Lord, dismiss your servant in peace. I've seen the Messiah.*

I know two things. Uncle Rob will soon be gone, and I'll never forget this touching moment.

The choir breaks into wonderful praise as Joseph and Mary reach the front of the auditorium. I'm reminded how music can move our soul like nothing else. It's such a precious gift from God.

Joe Aguillard is leading the choir. He's wearing an orange prison jumpsuit instead of his usual suit and tie. This year's musical is about Jesus being for everyone and each choir member is dressed as common people. There's a mailman, housewife with a mop and bucket, hard-hatted construction worker.

And Joe Aguillard, property of the Beauregard Parish Jail, leads it all. For nearly thirty years, Joe has been my best friend. He's stood by me through thick and thin. He's that faithful lifetime friend that is priceless.

Joe's strong voice soars above the choir as he sings with emotion and praise.

And for some strange reason I think of Carl Mosley.

Carl loved to sing as much as any member of our choir, but the fact is he couldn't carry a tune in the proverbial bucket. He was consistently off key.

There's a link between Joe Aguillard and Carl Mosley, and it's the heart of this story.

Carl and his family were the most faithful members of Dry Creek Baptist Church. The entire family once had perfect Sunday School attendance for over ten years.

The Mosley family was one of Dry Creek's most interesting families. Curtis Mosley, a large kindly man, was a World War I vet who'd later been a Texas Ranger. His wife, Lucille, was my beloved Sunday School teacher. Their two grown sons, Carl and John, lived at home. The entire hard-working Mosley family truly lived off the land, growing and producing practically everything they needed.

Carl was slightly retarded. He couldn't read and his speech was halting and slurred. However, he could take apart any engine and quickly put it back together in working order.

He and John supplemented the family income by cutting firewood and doing menial chores. They were something to watch at work. Even in their forties they could outwork men half their age.

Carl could sure cut firewood, but he couldn't sing well at all. I do not mean it unkindly, but Carl was by far the worst singer I'd ever heard. He had a dull monotone voice that was so off key it could always be heard above all the other singers.

So when Joe Aguillard came to Dry Creek as choir director, he inherited Carl Mosley.

Carl sang from his heart. I am confident that Carl's singing sounded "perfect to God's perfect ears."

But Sunday after Sunday, as Carl's bland monotone made "a joyful noise," it was more noise than note. It reminded me of the Andy Griffith episode where they tried to remove Barney Fife from the choir. That would have been a solution to Carl Mosley. Give him another job. Talk him kindly out of the choir.

But none of these things happened.

On choir specials, you could always pick out Glenda Hagan's soaring high soprano, Judy Aguillard's beautiful alto, the echoing enthusiastic bass of Donnie Reeves and my dad. All these voices blended in a beautiful way . . . but the indescribable sound of Carl's toneless voice hovered above them.

I once heard a recording of our choir's Christmas cantata. You could faintly pick out Carl above everyone else.

Being the 'song-less' son of a well-known singer, I know all about expectations and a little something about music. I've always been what is called a "funeral singer." When a full choir is needed for a weekday funeral, I'm happy to supply a warm body and a poor voice. I follow my wife DeDe's advice: if you forget the words or get off key, just keep mouthing "Watermelon, watermelon, watermelon."

Carl tied to get the words right. I'm sure he thought he was on key. Here's what I love about my best friend Joe Aguillard: there was never a word said about excluding Carl Mosley from the choir. His faithfulness was appreciated and his singing tolerated.

From time to time, choir members or church leaders suggested ideas on getting Carl out of the choir for the Christmas musical. Make him a shepherd of wise man.

However none of these suggestions made it past our choir leader Joe Aguillard.

Joe was, and is, a tremendous musician and leader. Everything he does is accomplished with quality and excellence. However, what I love best about my best friend Joe is his kind heart and compassion.

Helping the choir by *hurting* Carl Mosley was not an option.

In 1990, Carl died from a sudden heart attack at age fifty-two. Within two years, his younger brother John and their mother Lucille also died.

The long association of the Mosley family with our church ended. These were faithful members who *never missed* church and they were *greatly missed*. There are few traits better than faithfulness.

Now their pew was empty . . . Mrs. Mosley's red foot cushion disappeared. Carl's spot in the choir was vacant.

Regardless of whether the choir sounded better or not, we were all poorer for losing this special family of dedicated Christians.

Returning once again to today's Christmas musical, I scan the large crowd that has filled our nice new sanctuary. I realize that probably not one quarter of those present today would even recognize the names of Curtis, Lucille, John, or Carl Mosley.

But whether our present choir knows it or not, every person singing in this choir, and all of us enjoying it, is connected to Carl . . . . and Joe Aguillard's early years as choir director at Dry Creek.

Here is where I'm coming from: experience has taught me that God will give us *small tests* before He chooses to send us *major blessings*. It's as if He wisely says, "I'd like to give him this wonderful thing, but I'd better make sure he can handle it first."

I call these tests "matters of the heart." It is the time when we must choose between what the world would do and the right thing to do. These tests most often involve our dealings with people and relationships.

Jesus talked about this in several parables, especially in the story of the talents. We are all familiar with His oft-quoted words in Matthew 25:21: *"Well done, good and faithful servant! You have been faithful with a few things; I will put you in charge of many things."*

I firmly believe Carl Mosley (and his singing) was just such a test from God. It was a test to our church . . . and it was a specific test to our gifted music leader.

What was most important: a "perfect choir" or heartfelt singing from a simple man who could have easily been brushed aside? It was a test passed with "flying colors" by our church, our choir, and my best friend Joe.

The Christmas musical ends. Baby Jesus has fallen asleep in Tom's arms. Uncle Rob McCracken is also snoozing peacefully, leaned over on his wife Iola's shoulder.

I thank God once again for the gift of music—for how it allows us to come into His presence for communion, fellowship, and worship.

And I thank God for a music leader, who years ago listened with his heart and not just a musical ear.

As we age we naturally think more about heaven. It's because a lot more of the people we cherish are on that side of eternity. Wouldn't it be nice to know more about what being in God's presence is like?

Most Biblical references to heaven include singing and praise. The Bible talks of a heavenly choir singing before God.

Carl Mosley is in that choir.

He's not there because he was a good man, although he was.

Nor is he in God's presence because he probably didn't miss church five times in his adult life.

He is there because in his simple child-like mind he came to Jesus seeking forgiveness and new life. There are a lot of things Carl did not understand, but he had a clear view of God and His son Jesus as the way to Heaven.

In that heavenly choir, Carl Mosley's voice and key is perfect. He sings there with the same passion he sang with here. In the very presence of God he lifts up his voice.

In perfect tune and perfect communion with God.

> When we've been there ten thousand years,
> Bright shining as the sun,
> We've no less days to *sing* God's praise
> Than when we first begun.
> – Amazing Grace
> John Newton

GREEN TOMATO
MINCEMEAT
LUCILLE MOSLEY

---

2 GAL. (1 PECK) GREEN TOMATOES
2 T SALT
1/2 PECK APPLES, CHOPPED, 6½ LBS
5 LBS. DARK BROWN SUGAR
1/2 C VINEGAR
1 C SUET, FINE CHOPPED
2 T CINNAMON
1 T CLOVES
1 T NUTMEG
1 LB. RAISINS

- CHOP TOMATOES FINE
- DRAIN OFF JUICE AND MEASURE.
- ADD SAME AMOUNT OF BOILING WATER AS JUICE.
- ADD SALT AND COOK A FEW MINUTES.
- DRAIN AND ADD SAME AMOUNT OF WATER AND COOK AGAIN.
- DRAIN AND ADD SAME AMOUNT OF WATER AND COOK A THIRD TIME.
- DRAIN AND ADD REMAINING INGREDIENTS.
- COOK ALL TOGETHER WITH TOMATOES UNTIL THICK AND THEN CAN IN STERILIZED JARS
- USE 5 LBS PRESSURE FOR 20 MIN.

Helyn Green Aguillard has been a blessing to our community and state for ninety years. She is a Dry Creek girl who married Harry Aguillard and blended into the rich culture of Cajun Louisiana. My best friend, Joe, is her youngest son.

Crawfish Etouffee
Helyn Aguillard

1 . 16. crawfish tails
1 med. onion, finely chopped
Green onions, chopped
1 can Rotel tomatoes
2-3 cloves garlic
2-3 T roux
1 stick butter
1 med. bell pepper, chopped
Parsley, chopped
1 can tomato sauce
Salt
Black pepper
Cayenne pepper

Melt butter in pot on low heat.

Add onions, bell peppers, green onions, parsley, and garlic to butter and sauté 5-7 minutes.

Add roux and stir until all dissolved. Add tomato sauce and Rotel tomatoes.

*Let simmer on low heat for 10-12 minutes. Add crawfish tails and seasoning to taste.. Cover and cook 20-25 minutes. Serve over rice.

CHRISTMAS JELLY

Tractor Time

When this old world starts getting me down
And people are just too much for me to face.
I climb way up to the top of the stairs
And all my cares just drift right into space.
On the roof, it's peaceful as can be
And there the world below can't bother me.

– On the Roof
Carole King

We all enjoy the hustle and bustle of the Christmas season . . . but enough is enough.

It's so easy to hit overload during this time of year—It can be sensory overload or materially, nutrionally, too many lights, or too many commercials.

In the midst of this wonderful chaos, we must carve out a time and place to get away.

Carole King goes on up a New York City roof.

I get on my Dry Creek tractor.

Everyone—including you—needs something—or somewhere—where they can escape it all. A place where cares drift away, and relaxation slips in as a cool breeze.

My favorite place for this peaceful retreat is on a tractor. I climb aboard, prime the diesel engine and soon see the world from a different perspective. I get a more balanced and serene view.

I'm not sure how a tractor ride accomplishes this. It's probably in my country genes. Hooking my old Kubota tractor to a bush hog, disk, or box blade is all it takes.

Yesterday was a good example. It was a warm day for late December. My chore was plowing fire lanes around our tree farm.

Riding a tractor is even better when you're pulling a plow. There are few smells that lighten the soul like freshly turned earth. It's a smell God made pleasing for a man to breathe in.

106

Tractor time, as I call it, is something I need often, especially during the busy holiday season.

Do you make time for "tractor time?" You may not kowtow to the idea of riding on a chugging tractor. You may not even own one, or have a place to ride.

I've got friends with variations of tractor time—a thinking fire, rocking time, a long walk, or a long soak in a hot tub.

Another writer who cherished solitude, Henry David Thoreau, said it this way: "I'd rather sit on a pumpkin and have it to myself than be crowded on a velvet cushion."

Maybe there aren't pumpkins or tractors where you live. Like Carole King in New York City, you may have to find your solitude in a different place.

> When I come home feelin' tired and beat
> I go up where the air is fresh and sweet.
> I get away from the hustling crowds
> And all that rat race noise down in the street.
>
> On the roof's the only place I know
> Where you just have to wish to make it so.
> Oh, let's go up on the roof.
> At night the stars put on a show for free.
> And darling, you can share it all with me.
>
> I keep a-telling you,
> Right smack-dab in the middle of town
> I found a paradise that's trouble proof
> Up on the roof.
>
> So if this world starts getting you down,
> There's room enough for two up on the roof
> Up on the roof.

As you enjoy Christmas, take some tractor time, or roof time, or even a lonely pumpkin. It'll keep you sane and bring joy and perspective to your holiday.

A Danish Christmas
By Erik Pederson

One of Dry Creek's most memorable characters was Erik Pederson. He was a storyteller par excellence who always had a twinkle in his eye. Each Christmas, he'd share this story with me. I badgered him until he wrote it down and entered it in the *Beauregard Daily News* Christmas Memory Contest. It deservedly won first place.

It's a reminder of how America is a nation of immigrants, each with our own story to tell.

Of my many memories, the thoughts of my childhood family Christmas celebrations are among my favorites. In our home, we followed the Scandinavian traditions brought by my parents from their native country of Denmark.

Soon after my parents married in Denmark in 1923, they moved to the United States. They lived in Michigan where my father worked for the Pontiac Corporation. Later after I was born, we moved to New York. When I was nine we boarded a Pullman train for a long ride to a new home and life in a place called Lake Charles, Louisiana.

It was here in Southwestern Louisiana that I grew up with my many memories and happy times. Of these times, Christmas was a time I loved best.

Christmas was a special time in our home. On Christmas Eve, my father would place the large Christmas tree in the middle of the living room. As my two sisters and I watched, he would begin attaching white candles on the tree. This was accomplished by using straight pins to pin the candles to the tree limbs. My dad, being an engineer, decorated very carefully and evenly until the tree was filled with white candles.

While my father decorated the tree, Mother was in the kitchen preparing a special meal. When the decorations were finished, we'd sit down as a family for the traditional Danish Christmas supper of baked goose, rice pudding covered with grape juice, and Danish cookies and chocolate delicacies sent as gifts by our European relatives.

In the middle of the table sat a single wrapped present. As each of us looked at it, we silently wished it would be ours. This was the "almond gift." Mother placed an unshelled almond in the rice pudding. Whichever family member found the almond in their pudding got the present.

As children we didn't particularly care for the rice pudding, but the gift on the table would motivate anyone to eat it.

I still recall how my parents would both move their first bite of rice pudding around in their mouth as if *they* had the almond. Eventually someone found the almond in his or her pudding. As we finished the meal, my father would go into the living room and close the door behind him.

As we children helped Mother clean the kitchen, we knew exactly what was happening in the living room. Our dad was lighting the candles on the tree. When he had everything just right, we were allowed in to see the beautiful sight. There we would stand in our darkened living room mesmerized by the brightly illuminated tree. The sight of the green tree in brilliant white light was an unforgettable spectacle.

Dad kept a bucket of water by the tree, but I'm still surprised the candle-lit tree never burned down our house.

After a time of admiration we would form a circle around the tree and begin singing Christmas carols. As we walked around the tree, we sang the familiar songs such as "Silent Night," only we sang them in Danish.

Later as a teenager in Lake Charles, I always made sure the shades were drawn to the living room on Christmas Eve. I didn't want my friends to drive by and see me walking in a circle singing Danish carols.

At the end of each song, we would eagerly ask to open presents. But my father insisted on singing more songs as we circled the tree. He was a master at dragging out the Christmas Eve traditions.

When we had finally finished all of the songs, he handed out the presents one by one.

When the presents were finally all opened, my father would get out his Bible and read the Christmas story from Luke chapter 2.

I can still recall him clearing his throat before he started sharing the wonderful story of Jesus' birth. This is a tradition that he carried out in our extended family until his death. Today in our family, I carry out the tradition of this Bible reading.

Thinking back on these boyhood Christmas memories, I only began appreciating these special traditions when I became an adult. Christmas is still one of my favorite events. I enjoy every part of it.

In my mind I often go back to the "Danish Christmas" of my childhood.

I'm not sure Erik Pederson taught his wife Yvonne to cook Danish dishes. Yvonne, whose roots run deep in Dry Creek, is a wonderful cook who raised a houseful of hungry boys.

MANDARIN ORANGE CAKE
YVONNE PEDERSON

CAKE:
- 1 YELLOW BUTTER CAKE MIX
- 4 EGGS
- ½ C OIL
- 1 CAN MANDARIN ORANGES INCLUDING JUICE

FROSTING:
- 9 OZ. WHIPPED TOPPING
- 1 #2 CAN CRUSHED PINEAPPLE (DRAINED)
- 1 SMALL PKG. INSTANT VANILLA PUDDING

COMBINE ALL INGREDIENTS, BLENDING WELL. FILL AND FROST TOP & SIDES OF LAYERS.

KEEP REFRIGERATED.

Lazarus' Second Funeral

I guess I'm only one who attended both of Boaz Lazurus' funerals.

The second one was yesterday.

The first one was thirty-one years ago.

Folks around here simply call me "Rabbi." It's a name I like.

I remember Lazarus' funeral well. I was a young rabbi, only recently assigned to the Bethany synagogue. I'll never forget the raw grief of his two sisters, Mary and Martha.

I had grown to love the Lazarus family and spent lots of time with them in the days leading up to his death. It was like being on a storm in the sea. Up one minute, down the next. The sisters had such hope that The Teacher would come and heal him.

Martha, the older of the sisters, stood at the edge of town for two days waiting for Jesus to arrive.

He didn't come.

And Lazarus died.

Like the sisters, I questioned why the Teacher didn't come when summoned. He'd supposedly healed the blind and lame. He could've healed his dear friend.

But Lazarus died.

I helped with the preparation, funeral, and burial.

I was gone for a week after his burial. First Jerusalem then Jericho. On my way home to Bethany, I began hearing strange stories as I encountered travelers.

Jesus had raised a man from the dead.

A man from Bethany.

The rumors used many names. Boaz was such a common name.

It couldn't be him.

I had felt his cold body.

I had helped bury him.

Lazarus had died.

I hurried my pace as I neared Bethany, arriving late at night. The streets were empty. The Lazarus house was dark but I beat on the door.

Eventually, a lamp was lit.

Martha came to the door. "Rabbi, what is it?"

I hesitated. "Is it true what I've heard?"

"Come see for yourself." She led me to the very room where Lazarus had died. A man was sleeping, snoring softly without a care in the world.

"Lazarus, you've got company."

He rolled over, squinting at the lamplight, then sat up. "Hello, Rabbi."

I trembled and couldn't speak. It was like seeing a dead man. No, it was like seeing a *live* man who'd been *dead*.

For the next thirty years I served as his rabbi. In spite of my prodding, he'd never reveal much about what he remembered between his death and resurrection. He'd only wink. "You wouldn't believe me if I told you."

The rumors persisted about him. The most popular was that Lazarus had only swooned and came out of the grave when he awoke.

Lazarus was dead. I know a dead man when I see one.

Over the years, I officiated at many funerals attended by Lazarus, including his sisters—first Mary, then Martha. He grieved along with everyone else but there was always a far-away look in his eyes as if he knew something that made it all different.

Rumors swirled that Lazarus would never die. He shook them off. "Rabbi, I'm going to die soon but have no complaints. I had three decades of extra life."

Finally, last week he took sick and knew the end was coming. I spent time with him on his last day. "Friend, do you think Jesus is coming to rescue you again?"

"Yes, but in a different way."

I carefully broached a touchy subject. "Do you really believe Jesus is alive?"

"I know it."

"But you never saw him alive like some of the others claimed?"

"I didn't have to. He raised me. He had the power over death." Lazarus weakly tried to sit up. "Rabbi, what do you believe?"

"I believe He raised you from the dead."

"But do you believe He's the Son of God?"

"I'm not sure."

"What more proof could you need? Just believe."

They were the last words he spoke to me. He laid back, closed his eyes, and died early the next morning.

His nephews told me just before he died, he opened his eyes, reaching skyward. "I can see Jesus coming to get me."

Some may doubt it, but I don't. A wise rabbi once told me, "Which is most crazy: a person who hears thunder and says it was God speaking to them, or one who hears God speak and says it is only thunder?"

I've learned not to doubt belief.

Lazarus died the day before the Sabbath, so we hurriedly prepared his body for burial. It was a strange funeral to say the least. There wasn't much grief. It's hard to grieve for a man who was given thirty extra years of life and seemed eager to step into whatever lay on the other side.

It was more than ironic that Lazarus died on what the local Christians are calling the birthday of Jesus. I'm skeptical if they're very accurate about when he was actually born.

It's what they're beginning to call one of their two holy days.

The other one is the supposed day of his resurrection.

I doubt if their two holy days will ever be widely celebrated like our Jewish holidays or Roman ones, but the Christians sure observe them.

I can't get Lazarus' last two words out of my mind. *Just believe.*

I'm not sure I totally believe, but I do believe I'm closer.

It's difficult not to believe in the word and faith of a man who had two funerals. I always loved to hear Martha quoting Jesus' words from that morning of Lazarus' resurrection:

"I am the resurrection and the life. The one who believes in me will live, even though they die; and whoever lives by believing in me will never die. Do you believe this?"

—John 11:25-26

CHRISTMAS JELLY

A Gift from DQ

Christmas is a time for gifts, and there are all types of gifts.

The best gifts come from our hands and hearts. They are created through a strong combination of love and skill.

I'm obsessed with a gift I saw last week. I call it a gift from DQ.

DQ. I'm not referring to Dairy Queen.

I'm referring to Dwayne Quebedeaux.

Dwayne is a talented carpenter. His older truck sported a bumper sticker, "My boss is a Jewish carpenter." I admire Dwayne and his wife Allison for their commitment to helping others in the name of that carpenter, Jesus.

Two weeks before last Christmas, a need arose in Dry Creek. Harold Yancey died of cancer. His only survivor, his son David, insisted that his father be buried in a pine casket. "My daddy worked in the woods, and I want him buried in a wooden one."

That's fine and good if you've got plenty of money. Pine caskets are expensive at funeral homes and David didn't have the necessary funds.

That's when DQ stepped in. He volunteered to build a homemade casket for Mr. Yancey. He did a crash course on the size and style needed. A neighbor told me she heard Dwayne's router and table saw all weekend.

On Monday, Harold Yancey was laid out in the beautiful rough pine casket at our church. I watched his son's satisfied look as he examined the work of art—and gift of love—built by Dwayne Quebedeaux.

The entire community pitched in to help. Men from the Bible Church dug the grave. Dry Creek families provided food and sat with the body. Mr. Yancey's final journey to Dry Creek Cemetery was on the back of a log truck, not a hearse.

We'll see lots of nice Christmas gifts this week.

Some expensive; others simply crafted with love.

But none will match DQ's gift.
A pine casket built of love and rough pine.
Built from trees felled by Hurricane Rita's destruction.

It may seem morbid to feature a casket for a Christmas story.

We're much more comfortable talking about wooden mangers than pine caskets.

But to fully understand the *true* story of Christmas, we must realize that the *real* reason for the coming of the Savior was to die.

Jesus came for a purpose, and it was fulfilled with his death.

It's like the biker tattoo, "Born to Die." It was his purpose *and* destiny.

He lived a perfect life and died a sacrificial death.

He wasn't placed in a pine casket but in a rock-hewn tomb.

The best part of the story is that He didn't stay there. As proof of the fact that Jesus was God's Son and had completely retired our sin debt, God raised Him from that grave.

He's not in any grave, nor is He in any manger.

He is now seated at the right hand of His Father.

May you celebrate His birth as never before and serve Him *wholeheartedly* with every fiber of your heart, being, and soul.

Merry Christmas from the Creekbank. . .where good stories flow.

Creamy Nutty Fudge
Allison Quebedeaux

3 c sugar
1-1/2 cups Pet milk
3 T cocoa
1/2 c smooth peanut butter
1 c chopped pecans
2 t vanilla
4 t butter

Combine sugar, evaporated milk, and cocoa until smooth. Bring to a rolling boil and cook down. Stir constantly. Add peanut butter, pecans, vanilla, and butter. Stir until thick. Pour out onto a buttered surface, plate or counter whatever you prefer. Cut into squares.

Makes smooth, creamy candy.

CHRISTMAS JELLY

An Easy Mark

"I'm a thousand miles from anywhere, waiting for a train."
"Waiting for a Train" by Jimmy Rodgers

Calling someone an "easy mark" is normally *not* a compliment. We use it in the context of taking advantage of someone and associate it with weakness. I have a story that explains the term's origin. I'll let you—the reader—decide if being an easy mark is a compliment or not.

Thanksgiving and then Christmas are good times to think about the "G words" of gratitude and generosity. They're two of the best words in the English dictionary.

The Great Depression of the 1930's was a traumatic time in our nation's history. This is evidenced by how deeply affected those who lived through it were. My grandfather would sadly shake his head as he described the challenges of supporting a young family during that tough decade.

During these hard years, families and individuals were uprooted and roamed the country desperate for work. My mother, who was a young child during this time, told of sitting at the window of a moving train and seeing a hobo, hanging onto the side of her car, passing by.

Most hoboes were single men riding the rails looking for work. As the slowing trains neared a station, the hoboes would jump off and find the nearby gathering places called "hobo jungles."

One of my friends in Longville has a wonderful story from the Great Depression. His father was walking along the K.C.S. tracks toward their family home. Nearing their house, he found a note attached to a limb, "Next house: good eats."

He kept the note as a souvenir. He was proud to be an "easy mark."

The following is my favorite "easy mark" story.

An older widow lived along the tracks in a small Midwestern

town. Although alone and poor, this woman had a reputation for giving food to anyone in need. In the language of hoboes, she was an "easy mark."

Hoboes, using a piece of chalk or coal, would mark the gatepost or nearby fences of homes where handouts were readily available. This woman's gatepost was decorated with a massive X. She was used to the knocks at her back door, and actually looked forward to the opportunity to share, even though what she had was meager.

One winter, just before Christmas, a strong storm blew through her town. The pelting rain seemed to be coming down sideways, and soon turned to snow as conditions deteriorated.

The woman watched through her window as the slowing trains passed and wet hoboes jumped off, trotting toward shelter from the storm. However, to her surprise, they passed by her gate, oblivious to the cups of fresh hot soup awaiting them.

This disturbed her greatly as she watched the nearby tracks. When another group of men struggled by without stopping, she grabbed her umbrella and stepped out into the cold rain.

At her gatepost, holding her umbrella with one hand, she pulled out a piece of chalk and re-sketched her X where the rain had washed it off the post. Stepping back, seemingly satisfied that her "easy mark" was visible again, she returned to the house, wet but ready—ready and happy to greet the men who soon began coming through the gate to her door.

I love that story because I grew up in the home of "an easy mark."

His name was Clayton Iles, and he was my beloved father. Both of my parents modeled kindness and generosity toward others, but Daddy turned it into an art form. He was a true easy mark—always ready to give a helping hand.

Although not rich materially, he willingly made small "loans" to folks. Due to his being known as an easy mark, needy families came to him. And he helped willingly and without any expectation of repayment—which was good because repayment seldom came. He considered it a "gift" instead of a loan.

When he died, I stood by his casket for four straight hours

as a long line of friends and neighbors snaked out of the funeral home and into the street. Many leaned in and whispered about specific things Daddy had done for them—acts of kindness and compassion.

At Southern funerals and wakes, we use the term "come to pay our respects." That long line of mourners was Daddy's repayment on his giving—*respect mixed with love.* He chose to invest his life in others and it paid great dividends in the joy and friendship he received in return.

Beside his grave at Dry Creek Cemetery are several items: an old softball, a horseshoe, and a pinecone—all testaments to the things he loved. Engraved on his grave marker is the verse that was also engraved on his heart—the very words of Jesus in Matthew 25:35-40: ". . . For I was hungry and you gave me food; I was thirsty and you gave me drink; I was a stranger and you took me in; I was naked and you clothed me; I was sick and you visited me; I was in prison and you came to me. Assuredly, I say to you, inasmuch as you did it to one of the least of these my brethren, you did it to me."

That was his 'easy mark' verse. He viewed it as a commandment from his Savior and lived by it daily. Now I'm a long ways from being the man of generosity that my dad was, but I'm still working on it. I'm going to work on it extra hard this Christmas season.

Yes, Thanksgiving and Christmas are times when we remember it's better to give than to receive. A time to live with gratitude for the "easy marks" that show up on gateposts, in hearts, and in generous deeds.

My mother-in-law, Juanita Joyce Terry, known as Mammy to her grandchildren, was known far and wide for her baked beans. We'd search for her ceramic pot at family gatherings or dinner on the grounds.

"Mammy" was a delightful life-of-the-party lady. The first time I met her she climbed up in a Terry Hardware dump truck and drove it to a wedding shower.

Like my dad, Mrs. Juanita was an easy mark—the first to help in any time of need. She's famous for her reply to "Mrs. Terry, why don't you lock your house when you're gone?"

She smiled. "What if someone came to borrow something? They wouldn't be able to get in."

Mammy's Famous Baked Beans

1 large can Van Camp's pork and beans
1 lb. hamburger meat
1 large onion
1 cup brown sugar
3 tablespoons mustard
2 tablespoons Worcestershire sauce
2 tablespoons soy sauce

Brown hamburger meat.
Drain fat from meat.
Add meat and all other ingredients to the beans.
Place in a clay pot if available.
Bake at 325 degrees for approximately 45 minutes.

Bah Humbug Week

If you're still reading, and it's after Christmas, I'm impressed.

It's the week after Christmas and let's be honest:
We're sick of it all.
Glad it's over.
Too much of everything.

No matter how good our Christmas was, it wasn't as perfect as we imagined.
So, it's normal to have a post-Christmas letdown.
It's an emotional and physical hangover.

If we're not careful, it can be a spiritual letdown.
To help you through this weirdly wonderful week, we've included a short story for each of the seven days separating Christmas from New Year's.

The week after Christmas is a transition week.
I call it Inventory Week.
An opportunity to glance back at the past year.
A chance to look ahead to goals and dreams for the coming year.

So here goes, I hope you have a Merry . . ."Bah Humbug" Week.

Bah Humbug Week
Short List

1. Begin a gratitude journal. Daily write down one (or more) thing you're thankful for.
2. Give yourself a Scrooge/Grinch day. Then move on.
3. Develop a Life Plan for your coming year. You can read mine at www.creekbank.net/2012/08/my-current-life-plan/
4. Reflect on your blessings of the past year.
5. Do something for someone who cannot pay you back.
6. Write down your six words for the coming year. Here are my current ones:

    Passion
    Commitment
    Mentor
    Compassion
    Legacy
    Encouragement

7. Make and enjoy a pot of Ouiska Chitto Stew (next recipe).

For twenty-nine years, my parents owned and operated a canoe business on the Ouiska Chitto River. Weekends meant leaving at 7:00 a.m., working until dark, and coming home exhausted and hungry.

Mom was dedicated to ensuring her family was fed a hot and rewarding meal. Before we left for the river, she would assemble a large pot of beef stew in the crock-pot.

There was never a question of the menu for the long day; and after several years, we changed the name of her stew to "Ouiska Chitto Stew."

It has become a traditional name in our family, and Mom has left that legacy of dedication to her family.

—Kay Campbell Fox

Ouiska Chitto Stew
Marilyn Campbell

2 lbs. Stew Meat

6 Carrots scraped and cut into 2-inch portions

6-8 Potatoes peeled and cut into pieces

1 Onion

1 Bell Pepper

3-4 Stalks Celery

1 pkg. McCormick Beef Stew Mix

Seasoning to suit your taste

Brown stew meat in pan with olive oil and seasoning. Transfer meat to crock-pot and add remaining ingredients. Cook on slow for 8 hours. Serve with rice and cornbread.

CHRISTMAS JELLY

December 26

The Day After Christmas

It's the dusk on the day after Christmas. I'm hiding at the edge of Miller Pond, waiting for the wood ducks to come in.

You'd laugh if you saw me. I'm in camo and a dark ski mask. I'm sitting in a fold-up chair, trying not to move at all. It's time for the wood ducks to arrive.

Don't worry that I'm breaking the law and "roost hunting." I have no desire to shoot at the hundred or so ducks landing here. I'm here to watch them, listen to them, and just enjoy them.

These ducks know they are safe on the north end of Miller Pond. Five houses, including mine, surround the pond. No one hunts them, so they feel no danger when they come crashing in at dark each evening.

I've quietly slipped up on the pond and staked my claim to a spot to sit deathly still and watch the ducks arrive.

The wood duck is my favorite waterfowl. In my opinion, it's the most beautiful bird. The male drake is beyond description with its swirling palette of bright colors.

This evening, I'll have difficulty seeing their colors. Wood ducks arrive at their nightly safe roost spot as close to dark as possible.

The next morning they'll leave in a flutter of wings at the hint of daylight. They'll spend their day in creeks and ponds eating acorns and seeds.

This afternoon I felt drawn to the wood duck hole. It probably had something to do with it being the day after Christmas. Our family had returned from my wife's parents. All of our Christmas doings were over.

As always, I'd had enough Christmas to last me until next year for sure. In fact, I'll go ahead and be real honest: I'm glad the Christmas season is over. And I bet if you're honest, you'll agree that we all have Christmas overload by now: too much food, drink, eggnog, gatherings, music, etc.

It's time to return to the normal pace of life. I need to get outside and hear the wood ducks squeal.

This in no way diminishes that I've enjoyed Christmas. It is a wonderful holiday and I love every moment of it.

However, our body, mind, and soul can only take so much adrenaline, sugar-driven celebration. Now it's time to shift gears and return toward a more normal life.

My normal life is always re-discovered with being outside in nature. It's why I was drawn to visit the wood duck hole.

The great naturalist John Muir said it so well, "Come to the woods—for here is rest."

The first pair of ducks comes swooping in. They make a loud splash as they hit the water and swim about. They are quickly joined by others—mostly pairs, triples, and such.

A flock of four swings overhead. I love the beautiful sound of their wings jet-swooshing, tilting back and forth to slow their descent.

I always wonder how anyone could not believe in God after watching a bird fly.

The landing runway on Miller Pond is open with only small clumps of bushes and a few trees. The arriving wood ducks drop out of the sky, avoiding these obstacles as they splash to a happy landing.

Three ducks land thirty feet from my seat. It's too dark to see their colors but I catch their silhouette and recognize two as drakes by their larger hooded heads. They swim nervously in circles sensing my presence until they quickly disappear into the weeds.

There are enough wood ducks on the water now for the party to start—all manner of winging, flapping, squawking, squealing, and splashing. The drab-colored hens make the shrill eerie call that gives this breed its nickname of "squealers."

This squeal is hard to describe or replicate. I've used all type of wood duck calls—from store-bought to homemade ones, from shotgun shells and referee whistles. It's nearly impossible to replicate this sound of the woods.

The female ducks are calling loudly to the approaching flights of birds. It's as if they are saying, "Come on in, the water is fine." The approaching flocks call back.

The largest flock of the evening, eight birds, comes barreling in. They hit the water and I wonder where they spent the day after Christmas. Maybe on Monroe Harper's pond, on a slough in Dry Creek swamp, or in a rice field near Kinder.

The evening's wood duck traffic slows to a crawl, but I sit a little longer. A sense of serenity settles over my soul. It's as if I needed to wash the gritty grime of the busy holiday season off of my soul, and being among the wood ducks is a good place to begin.

Finally I fold my chair and leave. The ducks are quiet—they're getting ready for a good night's rest in the safety of Miller Pond.

After a lifetime of hunting wood ducks, I am just as satisfied to see them, enjoy them, and watch them. And why would I want to shoot at these Miller Pond ducks? If I did that, tomorrow evening's show would not take place.

Besides, they're special guests here, leasing space from Dan and Rose Manuel as well as Kenny and Marie Garst. It would be worse than rude to shoot a neighbor's ducks.

I walk among my pines on the trail home. These trees were planted six years ago and I'm amazed at their growth. It's muddy along the fire lane and my boots pick up the extra weight of the mud. I recall the lines of an old Marshall Tucker Band song,

"My idea of a good time is walking my property line
And knowing the mud on my boots is mine."

I love those words, but I'm very aware that I don't own this land. The bank and I own it together. In a few years, I do hope to have the deed on it, but even then I'll not really own it. It is just on loan to my family and me from the Lord. It really belongs just as much to the wood ducks, deer, and rabbits that live on it. They and their ancestors were here long before me and they'll be here when another family owns this tiny twenty acres that I so proudly call mine.

To the east, a full moon rises through the pines. I've been too busy with Christmas to observe what phase the moon is in. That's too busy.

I have one final chore for this day after Christmas. I've made a pile of limbs and brush in our fire ring. I light it and pull up an overturned tub as the fire builds up. My yellow lab, Ivory, nuzzles up beside me.

The full moon has now risen higher in the sky. It has lost its yellow glow and larger perceived size as it has risen higher. The quietness of the night, the fire, the warmness of watching the ducks—all serve as a catalyst to wash peace over my soul.

Lord, thanks for a great Christmas. So many blessings to count.

But Lord, thank you that this busy time is over.

It's time to return to a little sense of normalcy.

I can't think of a better way than to watch the ducks fly in.

"Who owns Cross Creek? The redbirds, I think, more than I, for they will have their nests even in the face of delinquent mortgages.

"It seems to me that the earth may be borrowed, but not bought. It may be used, but not owned. It gives itself in response to love and tending, offers its seasonal flowering and fruiting.

"But we are tenants and not possessors, lovers, and not masters. Cross Creek belongs to the wind and the rain, to the sun and the seasons, to the cosmic secrecy of seed, and beyond all, to time."

— Marjorie Kinnan Rawlings,
Cross Creek

December 27

Master

A man can have many dogs in his life, but normally there is one that occupies a special place in his heart.

For me, that dog was Ivory. A yellow lab with intelligent eyes and a perpetual smile, she graced our home for nearly fourteen years.

Ivory actually belonged to my son Clint but when he left for college, she stayed. She became my dog, or rather, she chose me as her master.

A few years later, Clint and I walked out of the camp office together. Ivory, grinning her silly smile, expectantly thumped her big tail against the wall.

I challenged Clint to a test, "Let's find out who Ivory really loves the most. You go north toward the road and I'll go east to the Tabernacle. We'll see who is her master."

He reluctantly agreed to my challenge. I was confident she would follow me because of how faithfully she always followed me each day.

We both agreed not to look back until we had reached our respective spots. As I walked the seventy-five feet to the Tabernacle, I expected at any time to hear her steps behind me.

Reaching the sidewalk I stopped and looked at Clint. He stood on his spot, the same distance from our starting point.

Ivory was sitting right where we'd left her, anxiously looking back and forth. She wagged her tail, grinning at both of us. She seemed to be saying, "Eenie, Meenie, Miney, Moe. . . ."

I walked to Clint. Ivory ran to us. I knelt and patted her head. "I'm sorry to do that to you. We won't put you in a bind like that again. You love *both* of us."

The words of Jesus came to me as I thought about Ivory's

allegiance. Jesus clearly stated that no man can serve two masters. In the Sermon on the Mount, He clearly spoke of allegiance and dedication, "No one can serve two masters. Either he will hate the one and love the other, or he will be devoted to the one and despise the other. You cannot serve both God and money" (Matt. 6:24).

The scariest part is this: many times, we stand and look back and forth at which master we will serve. The object drawing us away from God is often something good, but *anything* that blocks our commitment and dedication to God is harmful, no matter what it is. We must not settle for good when we can have the *best—an* intimate relationship with Jesus.

We cannot serve two masters. Just as Ivory whined at being unable to choose between her two masters, we are most unhappy when we are in the no man's land of attempted dual allegiance.

One more thought on choosing a master. We need a full understanding of what the word means.

I loved to hear T.J. Crosby pray. He used the endearing term "Master" throughout his prayers. It was his default address to God.

It's a good term.

Master. It says a lot.

I'm not sure I've ever heard anyone else use the term in their praying.

Master. It means Boss.

It's a subservient term, and we Westerners don't like being servile.

A person who exercises authority or dominates.

Doesn't sound like a sweet cooing baby.

It's easier to keep Jesus in that manger than to think of one who "directs and controls."

A victor who conquers.

Master.

It's a first cousin to the more familiar "Lord."

The finest example of the term *master* is in the gospels.

Let me set the stage. Simon Peter, a strong Galilean fisherman, has Jesus the carpenter in his boat. Jesus says, "Launch out into the deep and let down your nets for a catch."

Simon answers, "Master, we have toiled all night and caught nothing; nevertheless at your word I will let down the net."

The Jesus Film, based on the book of Luke, nails this scene. Burly bearded Simon looks confused, "But Master, we fished all night and didn't catch a thing." Then shrugs and smiles. "But if you say so, we'll do it."

There's a principle here: if someone is master, we'll obey him or her. We'll even obey them when it doesn't make sense. Sea of Galilean fishermen caught fish at night. Last night had been a waste. It didn't make sense to try again.

Other than that Jesus said it.

We remember the WWJD bracelets so popular in the 90s. "What Would Jesus Do?"

A lady made me a similar one.

DWJS. Do What Jesus Says.

Pretty simple. Pretty profound.

Secondly, when we know Jesus is our Master, we'll worship Him.

We'll bow in admiration, respect, and love.

That's hard for us Americans. It's in our blood to be independent—that attitude of "I'm no better than anyone, but no one's better than me." It permeates my culture in the piney woods of western Louisiana.

Our ancestors came here to be left alone. Not beholden to anyone.

But if we worship Jesus, we must bow to Him.

He's worthy.

He's worthy of our worship.

Finally, if we recognize Jesus as Lord and Master, we'll follow Him.

Go where He leads.

Strive to walk closely with Him.

Sometimes, the most miserable person in the world is not the person who has no room for God in his/her life. Yes, that person is unhappy and unfulfilled. However, there is probably no worse spot to be in than attempting to be both a follower of Jesus and the world. May we constantly be reminded of the love and grace of Jesus. Let us never forget His strong call for us to forsake this world and our own wants to wholeheartedly follow Him, this Amazing Jesus, the Son of the Living God.

Poor Ivory waffled back and forth between serving two masters. Often, I'm just like her, wanting to hang onto this old world yet reaching for higher things.

> *"Then choose for yourselves this day whom you will serve*
> *. . .But as for me and my house, we will serve the Lord."*
> —Joshua 24:15

I have so many fond memories of Ed and Kat King. They lived the Christian life in front of me—at church as well as at their dairy and the post office where Mrs. Kat worked.

I sat on the floor in their living room on a hot July night in 1969 as we watched man first step on the moon. "One small step for man. . . ."

I'm thankful for folks like the Kings who served as spiritual and surrogate parents in my life. For me Dry Creek was a huge extended family of kin, friends, and neighbors.

Banana Nut Cake
Kat King

2 . c cake flour
1 2/3 c sugar
1 t. baking powder
1 t. baking soda
1 t. salt
2/3 c. shortening
2/3 c. buttermilk
3 eggs
1 c. mashed banana
2/3 c. finely chopped nuts

Heat oven to 350°. Grease and flour oblong pan or 2 round 9-inch pans. Measure all ingredients into large mixing bowl. Blend 1 minute on low speed, scraping bowl continually. Beat 3 minutes at high speed, scraping bowl occasionally. Pour into pan(s). Bake oblong 45 minutes. Bake layers 35-40 minutes or until wooden pick comes out clean when inserted in center.
*I use butter cream frosting with finely chopped pecans added to it. Any fluffy white frosting would do as well.

CHRISTMAS JELLY

December 28

The 100-Foot Line

There's a fine stand of young slash pines at Dead Man's curve on the Longville Road. I've watched the growth of this forest since it was clear cut, then replanted in straight rows.

The following year, the pines began to poke their heads above the grass. They've emerged above the surrounding bushes and scrub trees. In the coming years, they'll link canopies, drop their pine straw, and completely wipe out the other growth in this field . . . *if a woods fire doesn't kill them first.*

I've been inspecting the fire lane plowed around these pines. With the approach of winter and its accompanying grass-killing frosts, having good fire lines is essential to protecting the young trees.

Woods fires often occur when a cold front and its accompanying north wind dry out the ground and grass. There is a long tradition of burning the woods among the folks here in western Louisiana's "No Man's Land." It began with the early cattlemen and sheepherders burning off the dead grass, believing that new fresh grass was better for their livestock.

Our native longleaf pines can survive most woods fires, but due to their slow growth, they've been replaced by newer species. The reforestation of Louisiana in the last eighty years has been with faster-growing loblolly and slash pines.

The trade-off is that these species cannot survive a hot woods fire. There's nothing sadder than a field of burnt dead pines, meaning a loss of trees and habitat from a fire.

For years, Southwestern Louisiana led the entire state in woods arson. The old settlers still believed it was their right to burn the woods.

Feuds over hunting leases or grudges led to "revenge fires." Sometimes the fires were accidentally set and spread by a strong wind and low humidity. Regardless of the source, our two most common species of pines are exceptionally vulnerable to fire.

I always worry over fields like the slash pines on the Longville Road. Once tall enough, they can withstand most fires. For the first five years or more, a hot fire will often destroy an entire stand.

That's why wise forest owners will plow a second inner "hundred-foot line."

This is insurance against the arsonist who tosses matches across the outer fire lane. This can stop the fire before it spreads to the entire pine plantation.

It provides insurance for the larger part of the field.

I see a spiritual and mental component to the hundred-foot line. In our busy lives, we need this guardrail of space and protection for our minds and souls. This fire lane, or margin, gives us boundaries and space to breathe.

It allows us to control the raging fires that can burn in our lives. I know all about that—I've had some hot fires in my own heart— usually self-inflicted.

How do we plow those hundred-foot lines?

Here are two ideas:

Be still. I love the words of the shepherd David in Psalm 46:10: "Be still and know that I am God." It's both a promise and a commandment. Taking time to be still, get quiet, pray, and meditate help us as well as protect us. We must build solitude and silence into our lives and guard a time and place for them.

Get outdoors. Wendell Berry made this statement, "The Bible was written to be read outdoors." There is something about being in nature: a clear blue sky, the wind in the pines, an owl's call, and a star-filled winter sky with a fingernail moon.

Get outdoors. There's something about being outside that is good for the inside of a man.

Be sure your hundred-foot fire lanes are in order. It's a lot easier to plow lines than replant pines.

December 29

Sharp Hooks

Reas Weeks was a Dry Creek legend who lived and died before my time. He was a bachelor who lived in a remote area along Bundick Creek. He never owned a vehicle or held a regular job. He supported himself by fishing, hunting, and farming.

He was known as the best creek fisherman in our area. My dad told the story from his childhood of the school bus picking Reas Weeks up. Mr. Reas flopped a forty-pound catfish on the bench by my dad. He was going to the general store to sell it.

Mr. Jay Miller, a neighbor to Reas Weeks, shared another story:

"I was always amazed at how Reas caught the largest catfish in Bundick Creek. No one else came close in size or quantity. One day I asked him how he did this.

"He led me to his barn and pulled out a large bucket with his hooks and lines carefully wrapped around it. He took a whet rock out of his overalls and began sharpening a hook. 'Jay, if you're gonna catch the big ones, you've gotta keep your hooks sharp. Those big catfish have tough mouths. A dull hook won't set, but a sharp one will.'"

It's a good story with a spiritual message:

Jesus has called us to be "fishers of men." If we are going to effectively reach others, our hook had better be sharp.

In my life I've found that this is only done by spending time with Jesus. As we study His word, the Bible, and fellowship with God in prayer, our lives will be sharpened for His use.

Yes, I never knew Reas Weeks . . . but one of his legacies is this story that I've shared dozens of times.

Wise words on sharp hooks from an old country fisherman.

Thanks Mr. Reas.

CHRISTMAS JELLY

December 30

Ready to Move Out

A few summers ago, DeDe, our youngest son Terry, and I took part in a youth camp in the Black Hills of South Dakota. This area of majestic mountains, covered with vast stands of tall Ponderosa Pines, is one of my favorite places in America.

To get to camp, we drove deeper and deeper into the Hills following a long snaking dirt road called Pasa Sapa Road (the Sioux name for the Black Hills). Upon arriving at Kamp Kinship, we were greeted by the friendly staff and soon made ourselves right at home.

One of the first things the Camp Director did was to instruct all drivers to park their vehicles outside the front gate. They were shown how to park in lines with the vehicles pointed out toward Pasa Sapa Road.

My inquisitiveness at this was answered by one of the local men. "Up here in the Hills a wild fire can spread quickly. During the hot summer season, dry lightning storms rake across this area. One lightning strike in these dry hills can spark a spreading dangerous inferno that destroys everything in its path." He nodded at the carefully parked cars. "We're ready to move out at a moment's notice. If you hear the camp bell ringing non-stop, it's the signal to load up and evacuate immediately. Don't even go back to your cabin."

This plan of "Being ready to move out" made an impression on me, especially later in the week. Wednesday evening, we had a wonderful worship service of singing and sharing. In the distant northwestern sky over the mountain, bright flashes of lightning split the sky one after another. My friend Stan said, "That storm's coming from Wyoming. This is just the type that sets off fires in the mountains."

About midnight the storm roared over the camp. There was no rain but plenty of howling wind, and bolts of lightning, and booming thunder.

Fortunately, no fires were ignited near Kamp Kinship. Only later did we learn that several fires erupted at different locations in the Black Hills.

Later that weekend we traveled into Wyoming to Devil's Tower and saw a huge wildfire that had been burning since the Wednesday night lightning storm.

Parking the vehicles pointed out at camp "ready to move out" gave me several thoughts about being ready. Here are a few:

Being ready to live. If only we would daily decide to live as if this was our last chance to suck in oxygen and see the sunset. Man, I want to be "ready to move out" and attack life with passion and joy.

Being ready to die. "No man is ready to live who is not ready to die." No one gets up in the morning and says, "Well, I believe I'll probably go out and die today." Deep down inside, we humans all secretly believe we'll be the one exception to the rule and live forever.

One time after the sudden death of a young person in Dry Creek, a wise man told me, "When you put your shoes on in the morning, you don't ever know who'll be taking them off you."

"Living, ready to die" for me entails living in a personal relationship with Jesus. He is my Rock, Friend, Savior, Confidant, and Guide. I've trusted Him for every aspect of my life, including my eternal destination. I can confidently face life *and* death knowing He is holding not only my hand, but also my destiny.

Living, ready to die also includes keeping a short account in my relationships with those around me. I choose not to let hurt feelings or a bad experience keep me from being in touch with others. If there is a problem, I go to them. As needed, I apologize and seek to make things right. That is a part of living joyfully and with gratitude.

I'm pointing the vehicle of my life so *I can be ready to go* ... or content to stay. Many of you have heard me speak of Brett Thornton who has a tattoo on each arm. One arm says, "R 2 G," and the other, "C 2 S."

These tattoos sum up his life mission: "Ready to Go, Content to Stay." It is an attitude of readiness to go where God leads: ready to jump in the vehicle and spin out if the bell of God's Holy Spirit rings out.

At the same time, it means possessing a quiet peace that we can trust God if our instructions are to stay put and dig deeper right where we are.

Ready to live.

Ready to die.

Ready to go . . . content to stay.

Always ready to move out when needed.

Moving up . . . and moving out.

CHRISTMAS JELLY

December 31

New Year's Eve

Finishing Strong

"If it's worth doing, it is worth doing right—especially if it is for God!"

Ted Williams is generally considered the greatest hitter in the history of major league baseball.

Two events from his career speak about the concept of "finishing strong."

In 1941, Williams entered the last day of the season with a batting average of .3995. This would qualify him for a rounded off average of .400 and make him the first hitter in seventeen years to achieve that mark.

His team, the Boston Red Sox, had a meaningless doubleheader that day, and by sitting out these two games, Williams could end the year at .400.

However that wasn't the Ted Williams way. He played in both games, and when the dust had settled, he'd gotten 5 hits in 7 at bats to finish with an average of .406. No one has hit above the .400 level in the seventy years since 1941.

Ted Williams retired at the end of the 1960 season at the age of forty-two. In his last at bat in the final game of the year, he hit a home run. Old news footage shows Williams rounding the bases with a skip in his step and joy on his face.

He hit a home run in his last at bat. That's finishing strong.

Finishing strong. We're remembered not by how we started, but how we finish.

Like Ted Williams, the Apostle Paul was a man of passion. He had an unyielding love for the Lord Jesus. In many of his writings, he expresses a strong desire to finish the work assigned to him by God.

Paul understood that *how we finish is how we are remembered.* Living in a day where his listeners understood about athletes, he compared it to striving to finish the race and win the prize. The first runner out of the blocks isn't always remembered. It's the one who finishes first.

Paul's words speak to this: "But none of these things move me; nor do I count my life dear to myself, so that I may finish my race with joy . . . " —Acts 20:24

P.S. One of my favorite anecdotes involves a baseball discussion:

"What do you think Ted Williams would hit if he were playing against today's pitchers?"

"Well, he'd be about ninety-four years old, so I don't expect he'd do too well."

January 1

Lagniappe

A New Year

Our wonderful Cajun culture has a unique word. *Lagniappe.*

It means something extra, and goes back to the rural tradition of shop owners giving faithful customers a little something extra as appreciation for their business.

Lagniappe. It's a good word.

It's a New Year.
We've woken up alive.
This is a new day.
It's Lagniappe.

It's a new start.
A special gift.
Lagniappe.

Enjoy it.
Suck the life out of it.
Squeeze out every drop.
Enjoy your lagniappe.

It's a New Year.

Being a writer, I always equate the first day of a new year with the blank pages in a new journal. As I open the notebook and leaf through its empty pages, the potential for what will be written and recorded there is limitless.

Being a journal keeper for nearly forty years has taught me several things. Some of this year's entries will be sad and painful. Others will be joyous and funny. That is the nature of life.

As the world enters this new year, the pages are blank and no human knows what this year holds. Never in my adult life have I seen such uncertainty and concern. From war and confusion in all corners of the world to an economic meltdown that has shaken the confidence of many, we face uncertain days ahead.

The year 1939 was much like that . . . especially in Europe. War had commenced with the German invasion of Poland and subsequent involvement of most of the continent's nations.

In England, the days were especially dark. It was in this bleak time at Christmas 1939 that King George VI made his annual Christmas message to the British people.

He quoted from a familiar poem by Minnie Haskins entitled, "God Knows."

> I said to the man who stood at the Gate of the Year,
> "Give me a light that I may tread safely into the unknown."
> And he replied, "Go out into the darkness, and put
> your hand into the hand of God. That shall be to
> you better than light, and safer than a known way."

The King's appropriate use of this inspiring poem stirred the British people, as it still stirs us over a half-century later.

It's a good poem as we enter an uncertain new year.

God is in control.

There is no panic in heaven.

As long as we hold onto His hand and follow His guidance, we'll be all right.

" . . . My God shall supply all of your needs according to his riches in Christ Jesus" (Philippians 4:19).

Epilogue

Honeysuckle

You won't find—or smell—honeysuckle during in January. A new year means there's at least two months before Southwest Louisiana bursts into spring and greenery. The fragrance of its pale pink blossoms is hard to describe. The "honey" in honeysuckle is the best way I know. It has a sweet pleasant aroma that once sniffed—like an endearing friendship—is never forgotten.

I began this book with a story of a beloved teacher, Eleanor Andrews, and her holiday gift of Christmas jelly. I've chosen to close it with a final story about this memorable woman.

Quietly, I ease into the ICU where Mrs. Eleanor Andrews lays surrounded by tubes and monitors. I'm holding a green vase of pink honeysuckle, and its fragrance has followed me down the hallway.

It's difficult to fathom that Mrs. Andrews will probably die during her favorite season of spring. I'd always thought she'd leave us in the dead of winter when the trees were bare and her garden was empty.

Her face is covered with an oxygen mask, but it doesn't hide the smile that's lit up my life since I was eleven. I lean down close because her voice is very weak. Most of what she says I can't understand, but I hear one thing clearly.

"I'm going home today."

For a moment I think she's confused and believes she's going home to Dry Creek. She reads my puzzled face and grasps my arm. "No, I'm going *home* today."

I understand. She's going *home* and looking forward to it.

She's suffered enough.

Most of the ones she loves best are already on the other side.

She's ready to go.

Nothing, not even her beloved flowers and yard in Dry Creek, can draw her to stay on this earth any longer. I hold her hand, unable and unwilling to let her go.

I recall a wonderful January evening last year in her home.

I brought nine boys, including my three sons, to watch the Division I Football Championship game. The boys, divided in loyalty between Virginia Tech and Florida State, were loud and enthusiastic . . . and in the midst of all this commotion, sat Mrs. Eleanor Andrews happily puffing away on a cigarette. I'll never forget the look of pure joy on her face. Her eyes seemed to glow from the enjoyment of being surrounded by young people having a good time.

We had such a swell time watching the game together—all eleven of us.

You can probably guess who enjoyed it the most—Eleanor Andrews.

Looking around on that special January night, I swear I could smell the fragrance of honeysuckle in her living room.

Maybe it wasn't honeysuckle, but the equally sweet aroma of love and friendship.

When the game ended, each boy came by her chair, leaned down, and gave her a hug. She kissed each one on the cheek. The sight of these country boys hugging on her touched me. She had lost two of her three sons to death, but for one precious night, her house was once again full of laughing boys.

I was at the end of the hugging line. She pulled me close with a surprisingly strong grip. "You'll never know how much this meant to me."

I couldn't speak. On that January night, I was too full for words.

🌲　🌲　🌲

Once again, I'm at her ICU deathbed.

Once again, I'm too full for words.

I lean down and kiss Mrs. Andrews on the cheek one last time and leave. I stop outside the cubicle for one final glance.

I see two things:

The smile on her face,

And the green vase of pink honeysuckle.

Mrs. Eleanor Andrews was wrong by one day. She died the next morning.

When I received the news, my heart was filled with a selfish sadness, but not grief. The suffering of her worn-out body had ended. Her long battle was over. I recalled the words of the Apostle Paul, ". . .Absent from the body . . . present with the Lord."
—II Corinthians 5:8
She was now at home with her God.

Eleanor Andrews was buried in Dry Creek Cemetery by her husband Red and sons Charlie and Keith.

Driving home, I stopped at the old Dry Creek School. It's where she attended school and later taught until the school closed.

I walked by her old fifth-grade classroom. There's nothing quieter or more eerie than an empty school building. This was the site of many of her happiest moments.

I was there for her final joyful day in this building. It was her seventy-eighth birthday party. She fussed at us for planning it without her permission. "No one is going to come. There won't be a handful of people come to see an old woman like me."

Sunday afternoon arrived and she was wheeled into the large conference room.

People kept coming—a long line of her grandchildren, country men who'd sat in her classroom, ladies who'd first been taught by her in Bible school, and old friends with whom she'd graduated from high school in this very same building.

When the party was over, she gave me her famous stare. "Come over here." She dropped her gravelly cigarette voice an octave. "Well, I guess I can forgive you now for planning this." She broke into a huge smile. "Today was one of the finest days of my life."

I walked out of the Old School sad and glad.

Sad at how we'll miss her in Dry Creek.

Glad our paths crossed on this journey called life.

I rolled down my truck window to let the cool March air in. As I crossed Mill Bayou, I noticed the honeysuckle blooms were gone for another year.

But deep down in my soul, I believed I could still smell the sweet and wonderful fragrance of honeysuckle.

I wonder if there's wild honeysuckle in heaven.

I sure hope so.

Postscript

2013 will be my first spring away from the aroma of wild honeysuckle.

I don't believe they're found in eastern Africa.

For the next several years, DeDe and I will be serving among the wonderful folks of a continent I've come to love, Africa.

It's bittersweet leaving our beloved Louisiana piney woods. It's the only home I've ever known. Well-meaning friends ask, "Why?"

Our answer is simple. This is what we strongly feel God is leading us to do at this stage of our journey. It's the right season *and* the right reason for us.

We're excited about the next part of our journey and the stories and growth that will result. We're sad to leave behind our families, friends, and especially grandchildren, but plan on taking all of these memories with us.

August Strindberg said it so well, "No matter how far we travel, the memories will follow in the baggage car."

Hop on board with us as we continue our journey. You can follow us at www.creekbank.net as well as our social media pages.

Most of all, we covet your prayer.

Thanks for joining us for a good helping of *Christmas Jelly*.

Writing for a reason,

Curt Iles
Dry Creek, Louisiana
Fall 2012

Curt is always ready to visit with book clubs through personal visits (when possible), Skype, E-mail, and Facebook. Please contact us at www.creekbank.net for more information.

Parents are encouraged to use these questions for nightly family time. Study groups and books clubs will also find discussion questions helpful.

Discussion Questions

Christmas Jelly
1. Why is a handmade gift always remembered?
2. What is your favorite jelly flavor and why?
3. Who was your favorite schoolteacher? Why?
4. What could we (family, book club, class) do to help our community?

My Grandpas' Boots
1. Who is the narrator?
2. What connection does the narrator have to both veterans?
3. What does this story teach about common ground?

Stolen Christmas Trees
1. Why does a stolen Christmas tree seem obscene?
2. How does one balance trust in human nature with common sense?
3. How does one's attitude affect our view on honesty?

Santa Claus is Coming to School

1. Representing Santa Claus is a heavy responsibility. What are some guidelines of behavior that a person must have if they are to properly represent Santa?
2. If you could choose any historical figure for a school substitute one day who would you choose and why?
3. Is using the Santa Claus image coupled with Schweitzer's glass eye story to present about God watching us, agreeable or bothersome?

What it Really Means

1. What sense of evolving relationship do you sense through Harry and Mr. Reed's conversation?
2. Is there a difference in believing in and believing about?
3. Does faith always involve action?

First Christmas in Dry Creek

1. What is your personal favorite story of kindness to strangers?
2. There are so many acts of kindness done during the Christmas season-*nursing home visits, collections of toys, and many others*. What is something your family could plan to do to show kindness after the Christmas season in over?
3. In our modern world, how do we differentiate between distrust of strangers (stranger danger) and kindness to strangers?

A Handmade Christmas

1. Why are the memories of simpler holidays so endearing?
2. What is your favorite childhood Christmas memory?
3. Describe a handmade ornament or two from your childhood.
4. Make a new handmade ornament with your children or grandchildren.

No Room at the Inn

1. What were your roles in past Christmas programs?
2. "Joseph" in the story thinks well on his feet. Is "thinking on your feet" an innate gift or can it be learned?
3. The real innkeeper gets a bad rap for turning Joseph and Mary away. However, he did offer them the stable. What do you think of his actions?

New Birth in New Orleans

1. Why is the desire to return to the place of one's birth/beginnings so strong?
2. There are many young mothers who are lonely and afraid in each of our communities. How can we help them?
3. Often New Orleans is labeled as "Sin City." What does this story tell you about the people of New Orleans and other areas that have such a reputation?

King of Kings, Lord of Lords

1. What is the funniest thing you've ever seen in church?
2. Have you ever been embarrassed by your family? How did you handle it?
3. Have you ever had to trust someone like Poppa did Fred?

On Forgiveness

1. Must one forget to fully forgive?
2. Why is praying for someone such a key on forgiveness?
3. Does forgiveness occur instantly or is it a process?
4. Why is it so difficult to forgive ourselves?

Buried Treasure
1. What's the first thing you think of when you hear "buried treasure"?
2. How are people like a buried treasure?
3. How can you look for a way to bring the shiny parts of people to the surface just as the coins shone after they were cleaned off?
4. Were you a "hidden treasure"? Who uncovered the treasure within you?
5. Take the time to write a letter of gratitude to that person or their children.

Medic
1. Why does killing during the Christmas season seem so obscene?
2. Is courage always free of fear?
3. Are you familiar with other wartime Christmas stories?
4. Have you had a target in sight but were prompted to back off to wait and see?
5. Which character do you relate to most?

The Warm Glow of Giving
1. Why does the American view of retirement often leave retirees feeling useless?
2. Why does it always affect our spirits to give to others?
3. What does it mean to "get outside oneself"?
4. As a group, find a place to share the warm glow of giving this season.
5. What keeps Mancel and June going even through sickness and retirement?

Hardest Day of the Year
1. What's the most difficult Christmas you've faced?
2. How did you get through it?
3. What are signs that someone may be struggling during the Holiday season?
4. Have you ever been the gift bearer to one having a hard Christmas?
5. Try this season to seek out one who may be hiding their pain.

An Old Feed Trough
1. Why do we often "sanitize" the manger scene?
2. Why is self-effacing humor so attractive? "I . . . fall on my butt."
3. What are simple symbolic items in your family's Christmases?

Too Much Jesus
1. Why does the name of Jesus often offend others?

Hay's in the Barn
1. Why is there such satisfaction in finishing a job?
2. Can you identify with the author's rural examples?
3. What will you put on your "hay in the barn" list?

The Heavenly Choir
1. How did the choir director show his love for people?
2. What does it say about how a person treats someone with a handicap?
3. Why is "Amazing Grace" such an endearing song to Americans?

Tractor Time
1. Why can Christmas be so frustrating?
2. How do you find "tractor time" for your sanity?
3. Why is Carole King's "Up On The Roof" such an enduring song?

A Danish Christmas
1. How does the storyteller use humor in this story?
2. Why is it important to celebrate ethnic traditions in our Christmas celebrations?

Lazarus' Second Funeral
1. If you could've talked with Lazarus, what would you have asked?
2. How would you describe the narrator's view of who Jesus is?

A Gift from DQ
1. Why was this gift so important?
2. How does the statement "Born to Die" relate to Jesus?

An Easy Mark
1. How do we balance being generous with being taken advantage of?
2. Why was the man proud of the "Next House: Good Eats" sign pointing to his house?
3. How would you describe the personality of the woman going out into the storm?

Bah Humbug Week
1. Why do we often feel washed-out after Christmas?
2. Is it normal to feel a post-Christmas let-down?
3. What would you place on your "Bah Humbug" short list?
4. What would be your six words for the coming year?

The Day After Christmas
1. What are ways you recover from the Christmas season?
2. Why is being out in nature a good antidote for the Christmas blues?
3. How does Rawlings' "Who Owns Cross Creek" relate to the wood duck story?

Master
1. Why does the term "Master" often bother us?
2. Why do dog stories like Ivory connect with our hearts?

The 100-Foot Line
1. What lesson is the writer trying to impart?
2. Why is it often so difficult to slow down?
3. What are the results from slowing down?

Sharp Hooks
1. How would you describe Reas Weeks?
2. What was the key to his fishing success?
3. What life lesson does this chapter teach?

Ready to Move Out
1. Have you ever had to evacuate your home? Why?
2. What would you grab if you suddenly had to evacuate your home?
3. What life lesson is in this story?
4. What does it mean being "ready to live or die"?

Finishing Strong
1. Why is starting not as important as finishing?
2. What can you tell about the character of Ted Williams?
3. In what areas of life do you wish to finish strong?

Lagniappe: A New Year
1. How do Louisiana Cajuns use lagniappe?
2. What is so refreshing about starting a new year?
3. Why was King George's quoted poem so timely to the British people?

Honeysuckle
1. Re-read the opening chapter "Christmas Jelly." How does "Honeysuckle" compare with it?
2. Why do childhood teachers remain special to us? Who were your favorite teachers? Why?

On Leaving the Piney Woods
1. The author uses the term "bittersweet." What does that mean?
2. What does he mean by "the right season and the right reason"?
3. What season of life are you in?

ACKNOWLEDGMENTS

Finishing a book is a team effort. No one crosses the finish line unaided. I've been fortunate to be surrounded by a team of folks who help, guide, and encourage my writing.

Thanks to Ashley Miller for her input. As always, her parents Mark and Kari Miller are an integral part of my writing.

It's a pleasure working with my personal assistant, Judi Reeves. She and her husband Donnie are my friends as well as co-workers.

Julian Quebedeaux lends his artistic eye to my books. Jade Ross, my illustrator for Uncle Sam, also helped. My new friends, Ethan and Taegan Reiters, have been involved.

Paul Conant of Dallas is an excellent editor. If there are any errors in Christmas Jelly, it is in spite of his hard work. I also appreciate Julie Johnson and Joy Pitre for their eagle eyes.

My Uncle, Bill Iles. has his fingerprints all over *Christmas Jelly*. He has been a lifetime encourager and mentor.

Special thanks to my Mom, Mary Iles and sweet sisters, Colleen Glaser and Claudia Campbell.

My agent, Chip MacGregor, and mentor, Diann Mills, are sources of inspiration and wise counsel.

My friends at Sycomm Publicity, Stephanie Ryder and Pat Fox, have helped us spread the word of our books and speaking. Thanks ladies!

To everyone who contributed recipes, thank you!

I appreciate Ruth Taylor and the Ritchie Young family as well as the "Biggie" Spears family. The spirit of forgiveness in your stories will touch lives.

My best friend and wife, DeDe Iles, is always a key to everything I do, including writing. She has encouraged me to pursue my dreams.

Bibliography

King, Carole and Gerry Goffin. "Up on the Roof"
copyright 1962 Screen Gems-EMI Music Inc.

Marshall, George and David Poling. *Schweitzer: A Biography.*
(Doubleday, 1971) 174.

"The Jesus Film" © 1995-2012 The JESUS Film Project®

A Ministry of Campus Crusade For Christ International®

Marge Rawlings *Cross Creek*
copyright 1941 Simon and Schuster Inc.

Minnie Haskins   "God Knows"
The Gate of the Year Public Domain

Toy Caldwell "Property Line" Capricorn Records
copyright Spirit One Music BMI

Pictorial gallery and story backgrounds

Other Books by Curt Iles
Historical Fiction:

A Spent Bullet
ISBN: 978-1-4497-2233-3

The Wayfaring Stranger
ISBN: 978-0-9705236-9-6

Uncle Sam: A Horse's Tale
ISBN: 978-0-9826492-3-7

A Good Place
ISBN: 978-0-9826492-1-3

Short Story Collections:

Deep Roots
ISBN: 978-0-9826492-0-6

The Mockingbird's Song
ISBN: 0-9705236-4-5

Hearts across the Water
ISBN: 0-9705236-3-7

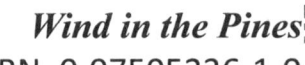

Wind in the Pines
ISBN: 0-97505236-1-0

The Old House
ISBN: 1-4033-5227-5

Stories from the Creekbank
ISBN: 0-759-69895-3

*Books are also available in e-book formats at Amazon.com
and Smashwords.com*

Curt Iles writes from his hometown of Dry Creek, Louisiana. The author of eleven books, Curt celebrates the history and culture of Piney Woods Louisiana in his writing. To learn more about his writing and speaking, visit www.creekbank.net.

Curt is represented by Chip MacGregor of MacGregor Literary Agency

Ashley Miller is a student at East Beauregard High School and is an eighth generation of western Louisiana's unique piney woods region. She lives in Dry Creek with her parents and brother and sister. Ashley compiled the recipes, discussion questions, and served as editor of *Christmas Jelly.*

Julian Quebedeaux is a film graduate of the University of New Orleans. A Dry Creek native, he designed the covers and organized the interior of *Christmas Jelly*.

He can be reached at: thaninja101@gmail.com

Judi Reeves serves as personal assistant to Curt Iles and Creekbank Stories. She and her husband Donnie live in Dry Creek, Louisiana. In addition to handling all orders and bookings for Curt, she loves being a grandmother and a good neighbor. She can be reached at jaycee52003@yahoo.com.

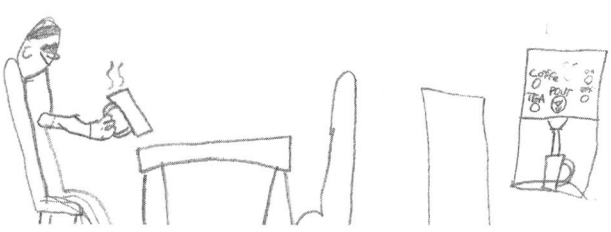

"The Joy of Christmas Jelly"
By Ethan Reiter

-73-

Curt,

I hope you use this book as if it were a silent friend— something to confide in. Write down your personal observations about the world around you... whether it is something specific, like the fragile mystery of a spider's lacelike web or something general like "all people are interesting-sometimes. But write—
don't worry about sentence structure, or punctuation or anything else — invent your own way of putting it down —

But write.

Write about the things that turn you on — the things you like — the thing you love And also write about the pain you see and feel — the things that upset you or disturb you. In writing these things down in this, your book, you will be discovering parts of yourself that lie deep within, next to the soul of your being... and also discovering parts of the awesome sacred mystery of life — and the beauty of words. The more we feel (both joy and p the more we are ALIVE and COMPLETE as human beings.

In this journey we call life you have, so many wonderful attributes that give you an advantage and will mark you as a leader— your courage, your spiritual awareness, your high intelligence, your sensitivity to the needs of others, your grand sense of humor and your youth...
It is an interesting and mighty adventure and you will go far.
With my love I offer you these blank

Bill Iles' note in Curt's first journal circa 1973.
See page 38 for corresponding story.